Bloody Bonds

A RACE AGAINST DEATH

A COLOMBE BASTARO MYSTERY - VOLUME III

NINO S. THEVENY
SÉBASTIEN THEVENY

SELF-PUBLISHED

© Nino S. Theveny, 2022-2024

The French Intellectual Property and Artistic Code, as set forth in sub-paragraphs 2 and 3 of Article L.122-5, only allows, on the one hand "copies or reproductions strictly reserved to private use of the copier and not for collective use," and on the other hand, "analyses and short quotations serving as examples or illustrations". "Any representation or integral or partial reproduction, without prior written consent from the author or his or her beneficiaries is deemed to be illegal" (sub-paragraph 1 of Article L.122-4). Such representation or reproduction anyway whatsoever, shall be sanctioned by Articles 425 and following of the French Penal Code.

Translated from French to English by Jacquie Bridonneau
Original title: *Mariage Mortel*

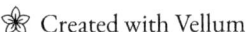 Created with Vellum

For Nenette, my dear granny, my surrogate mom, someone I would have preferred to see in the first place in her race against death.

Prologue

DEAR COLOMBE, *Blessed Jerome,*

Please allow me to begin by congratulating you for your marvelous wedding. That ceremony was a complete success and a moment of grace.

But the time for rejoicing is now behind us.

Now it's time to set your watches and begin the final countdown.

You both like playing games, don't you?

You even think you're pretty good at them?

You're sure you can solve any enigma?

It's true, Colombe's sagacity proved its worth a couple of years ago in Nice, with the Lacassagne family and its "one too many brothers."

Also true that you solved that "perfect crime" in Gwada...

But all that was mere child's play faced with what I'm now proposing!

As of today, you'll have to call upon your gray matter like never before.
To prevent one of your 99 guests invited to your moving wedding ceremony from dying...
Except I won't be telling you WHO nor WHEN nor HOW...

Danger will be lurking everywhere and all the time, around any of them.

99 potential victims.
    99 people in danger.
    99 reasons to tremble.

How can you save them? By solving my enigmas...
    Ready? Go!
    Tick tock, tick tock, the countdown has begun.

The race against death can now start...

CHAPTER 1
The chamber pot

FOR THE FIRST time since I'd met Jerome, I decided to pick up my pen and write our story, our adventures. Up till now, because of his experience and his appetite for writing, he'd been the natural narrator. He was the one who had reported upon the mind-boggling fate of the Lacassagne family in Nice, then that ghastly story that had unraveled during our vacation in Guadeloupe.

This time though, it seemed to be evident to me that I would be the one telling you the following tale. It had touched me so very closely that I didn't seem to have a choice.

Just a few hours after what should have been engraved in our hearts as one of the most unforgettable moments of our lives, we slid from utter felicity into sheer horror.

How could we bear so many terrible events when we'd just said *I do* in front of our friends and family?

In other words, how to go insane right after getting married...

Those were the questions we were asking ourselves the day after we'd tied the knot.

Yet, everything had started off so well.

IN THE MORNING, the few guests who had partied with us till the break of dawn came to wake us up where we were hiding in a place that was a secret for everyone, except for Sara, my sister.

A couple of hours earlier, Jerome and I had snuck away from our reception venue, after having finished the "compulsory figures" such as the first dance as man and wife, cutting of the wedding cake and making fools of ourselves singing karaoke. My feet were boiling in my brand-new shoes because of too much dancing, my bun and hairdo were starting to irritate me because it was so tight, and my eyelids had begun to droop with fatigue and too many glasses of wine. It was now time for our wedding night. I'll spare you the details of those short hours of shared intimacy and will fast forward directly to the moment when we heard muffled voices behind the shutters of our room. A handful of night owls, both family and friends, were visibly getting ready to roust us out of bed for the always hilarious episode of the "chamber pot!"

My eyes still half closed, I gazed out from our room to see our friends Laurent and Melanie, Fabienne and Marc, as well as my cousins Bertrand and Pascal, Aunt

Clarisse and Uncle Eric, her husband. Jerome's parents, Joao and Maria, had also danced till late at night as had my eighty-eight-year-old grandmother, Suzanne, who had insisted on taking part in the festivities nearly to the break of dawn, until she was driven back to the senior residence where she now lived.

I HAVE no idea if this is a tradition all over in France nor even if everyone has heard of it, but I must admit that for me, it was a first... and quite an unprecedented and unsettling experience.

Plus they had all outdone themselves so that chamber pot — and authentic one that had belonged to my great grandma — looked completely true-to-life and natural. The porcelain basin, chipped here and there, had been filled with a foamy yellowish liquid that I identified as being champagne, with melted and hardened chocolate artistically placed on the rims in suspicious looking flows and a couple of pieces still stuck on the bottom of the pot. They had even gone so far as placing a few sheets of pink toilet paper, the ultimate in poor taste, on one of the edges. Yet they were expecting and encouraging Jerome and I to sip a few mouthfuls of that horrible looking beverage. And all that at seven in the morning, our stomachs still stuffed from a night of feasting and festivities. Just imagine the ordeal!

Now, writing these lines, I can still see Jerome's nauseous wince, his trembling lips on the edge of the chamber pot, getting ready to swallow the mixture, encouraged by the dozen or so of our guests who had prepared all of this. They were hilarious, laughing, and all belting out *99 Bottles of Beer on the Wall*, to accompany us. And Auntie Clarisse who shouted out "*That's disgusting!*" with an unforgettable air of satisfaction and contentment on her face.

Yes, it was disgusting! Yes, it was both an atrocious and joy-filled moment!

Ah! I would have liked those instants of joy to continue, instead of turning into a nightmare just a few hours later…

CHAPTER 2
The urn

THE NEXT DAY flowed by at first like a peaceful and enchanted river.

We had lunch enjoying leftovers from the night before with a good third of our guests. We all danced a bit too, more at ease in our everyday clothes than in our wedding attire.

Then it was time to say goodbye, with our guests leaving to go back home, to their part of the city or country, back to their daily lives.

That evening Jerome and I were alone, exhausted, but euphoric and elated. We weren't hungry and just had a few bites of various fresh salads the caterer had prepared. Our heads were full of memories, emotions and impressions. Happiness as we'd seen so many friends and family members in such a short time, we'd all laughed, danced together, people of all ages, young and old, mixing extroverts with introverts. An unforgettable wedding, our wedding.

Our hearts overwhelmed, we decided to open the urn we'd put in a corner of the venue so that our guests could slip in a card, letter, something serious or funny, whatever they wanted.

We were spoiled rotten, congratulated, thanked, encouraged to start a family right away, though this was something we hadn't even thought about. Dozens of envelopes to open, discover, read, appreciate.

AND SUDDENLY... THE envelope!
The one that cut our legs out from underneath us, petrifying our hearts and souls.
The one that we wished we never had opened.

THE ENVELOPE itself was quite ordinary. Like most of the others, our first names were written on it. Nonetheless, something that could have surprised us and that we didn't pay any attention to after having read it was that they were not handwritten, they were typed.

Just like the sheet of paper that was folded in three parts in the envelope.

The letter began pleasantly.
My Dear Colombe, Blessed Jerome,
Please allow me to begin by congratulating you for your marvelous wedding. It was a complete success and a moment of grace.

But right when we read the following sentences, our mouths dropped open.

But the time for rejoicing is now behind us.

Now it's time to set your watches and begin the final countdown.

What the heck was going on? What followed, a series of three questions for us, completely blew us away.

You both like playing games, don't you?
You even think you're pretty good at them?
You're sure you can solve any enigma?

Good Lord, why all those questions? They didn't have anything to do with our wedding. What followed though unfortunately was quite similar.

It's true, Colombe's sagacity proved its worth a couple of years ago in Nice, with the Lacassagne family and its "one too many brothers."

Also true that you solved that "perfect crime" in Gwada...

But all that was mere child's play faced with what I'm now proposing!

No doubt about it, the author of those words knew what we'd done in the past. What was that person going to "*propose*" to us? We couldn't help ourselves from continuing to read. But then, our hearts both burst open in unison!

As of today, you'll have to call upon your gray matter like never before.

To prevent one of the 99 guests invited to your moving wedding ceremony from dying...

Except I won't be telling you WHO nor WHEN nor HOW...

Danger will be lurking everywhere constantly, around any of them.

99 potential victims.
99 people in danger.
99 reasons to tremble.

That was absolute horror! Was this someone trying to play games with us? But who would be capable of concocting a sick joke like that?

The deathblow hit us at the end of the letter, seemingly confirming that this was not a game, but rather a real threat.

How can you save them? By solving my enigmas...
Ready? Go!
Tick tock, tick tock, the countdown has begun.
The race against death can now start...

My hands shaking, I dropped the sheet of paper on the couch where we were sitting to go through the urn, which logically should have only contained letters of congratulations and good intensions.

"What the fuck is this shit?," swore Jerome with a scratchy and angry voice.

"Why? Why do something like this to us, now?" I murmured while sputtering. "Do you think it's serious?"

"Well, if it's a joke, it's got pretty poor taste, don't you think? I can't imagine anyone being capable of something horrible like that."

We held each other in our arms on the sofa, our

hearts heavy and souls ripped apart by that absurd threat, one that was even more inappropriate in these circumstances.

Who would dare threaten us the day after we got married? Who could be crazy enough to inflict something like that on us?

Thoughts were silently racing through our minds. It was Jerome, my husband since yesterday — I would have to start thinking of him like that —, who interrupted our cogitation.

"The man or woman who wrote this would have to have entered the banquet hall at some time to put the envelope into the urn. We must have seen them. It's horrible."

"That means that it is potentially a family member or one of our friends."

"Nothing's sure and everything's possible. This is what we'll have to find out."

CHAPTER 3
Looking elsewhere

THERE WAS no way in our opinion that someone we'd invited to our wedding could have done something so ignominious. How could we believe that a brother, a cousin, an uncle, a grandmother, who knows, could think it would be fun — but what an awful sense of humor! — and do something so abject and heinous? I began to think aloud.

"First of all, this person would have to have a minimum amount of knowledge in IT. Know how to write a letter using Word, lay it out, print it."

"Plus printing our names on an envelope, which means they'd have to know how to adjust the parameters in the printer," Jerome aptly added.

"And that would eliminate the boomers. For example, that's something Suzanne wouldn't know how to do."

The image of my grandma, a French version of Miss Marple in her senior residence, in front of a PC typing that horrible letter made us smile, despite or perhaps because of the tension squeezing our chests.

"I can't imagine a relative or a friend doing that to us," hissed Jerome. "It's impossible! Can you see your father or mother or your sister doing that? No, frankly, I think we have to look elsewhere. There were loads of people who came in and

out of the reception hall, either under our eyes or maybe that person even snuck in."

"That's crazy, who knows, maybe we saw the author of this letter putting the envelope into the urn, right under our eyes, while smiling at us!" I suddenly realized. "That's Machiavellian. Who are you thinking of?"

"We'll have to draw up a very precise list of everyone who was in and out of the banquet hall yesterday, beginning with cocktails and ending with lunch today at noon! And there were lots of people. We had ninety-nine guests for the meal, but how many people were hanging around outside while the doors were open just so they could access the restrooms or hang up their coats?"

I nodded, regretfully.

"A hundred and thirty?"

"Yup, probably easily that many. And that's without counting the staff members, and we can add the DJ, the photographer, the mayor, the priest..."

"No! Not the priest, come on!" I interrupted. "Stuff like that isn't Christian..."

"It isn't, but we can't rule out anyone for the

moment, unfortunately. We have no idea who's being targeted in the group of ninety-nine potential victims, but even more importantly we have no idea who could have been the author of those threats amongst the hundred and thirty or so people who were near our urn for two days and one night."

"We can eliminate the children, can't we?"

"Till the age of fifteen then. Don't forget that there are more and more kid IT geniuses. And nowadays, because of TV series or social networking, we know how the psyche of kids can quickly veer to the dark side. Child killers are always on the front pages now…"

I shivered just thinking about that.

"You're bullshitting me, it's no laughing matter."

"I'm serious," Jerome insisted.

"So you mean that everyone could be guilty or be a victim… That's the worst situation ever… Or how to shift from extreme happiness and bliss to tragedy in a mere twenty-four hours…"

I leaned up against Jerome's comfortable shoulder, he slowly ran his fingers through my hair and kissed me softly on my forehead.

"What are we going to do now?" I asked in a weak voice.

"I don't think that we'll be able to get to the bottom of this alone this time. We're going to have to go to the police."

"They're going to make fun of us if we waltz in with this bunch of baloney," I hesitated.

"I think on the contrary that we're going to have to take this warning very seriously."

CHAPTER 4
In memory

WITH A BIT OF APPREHENSION, but also with an ounce of hope, we went to the police station with that typed letter and its envelope.

Captain Vincent Delahousse, a tall Scandinavian-looking blond guy, came out to talk to us. He asked us to give him all the details of everything we could think of since we started decorating the banquet hall up until we opened the envelope. Which is what we did, Jerome and I, according to our respective memories. And talk about complicated! Asking a couple of newlyweds what they remember about the days and hours before their wedding! Our minds were monopolized by those last-minute little organizational details at that time, and we weren't focused on anything else.

Yet, we were able to satisfy the captain without him laughing at us. Then he began to ask us questions.

"And you're absolutely sure that this couldn't be some sort of sick joke that a friend or family member is playing on you, someone who likes to joke around, even when it's in poor taste? In everyone's families there are hellions like that who sometimes don't even realize how stupid they are or how much they can hurt someone."

"This letter doesn't seem like a joke to us, Captain. It could have been, of course, if he had added some smileys around the text or something like that," Jerome said ironically. "Or at the end he..."

"Or *she*," the policeman cut him off.

"Or she, if you want... she had written something like, *Haha, guess I really creeped you two out! I was just joking. Love you and be happy*, and then signed it with his or her first name. But here it seems pretty clear to me. The person who wrote this is presenting us with a challenge, and if we fail, someone we love is going to die!"

"Have you got any idea who could have written this? Does anyone that you know have any reason to hurt you? Have you recently had arguments or problems with anyone? During your wedding party, did any of the guests get into a fight? Maybe it would be a good idea to start off by trying to find the reasons for a letter like this, their origins. Ask the right questions, meaning, start off with yourselves, you who the letter was sent to. Do you have something to reproach?"

I could feel Jerome tensing up. He exploded.

"I don't believe it! Pretty soon you'll arrest us for encouraging and inciting violence! Dammit, why would people that we love, who love us, who are our friends or family members and who we wanted to join us to celebrate our wedding — and it was a great and happy wedding, let me assure you —, want to harm us, either us or any of the guests?"

Captain Delahousse put his muscled forearms on his desk, joining his hands together in a gesture of peace.

"Please, Mr. Bastaro, calm down. I understand what you're saying and am not doubting the authenticity of this letter. But there's a huge chasm between threats and actions. You have no idea how many cases like this we have every year and which, luckily, don't have any fatal consequences."

I frowned, annoyed, and this time I was the one asking a question.

"So what should we conclude? That you're not going to raise your little finger to help protect these potential victims?"

"Miss Dechamps, excuse me, Mrs. Bastaro, I'm going to be very transparent in my answer. Do you sincerely believe that we have enough police officers to ensure the protection of a hundred or so people of all ages, and living all over France and maybe abroad? Because, like the author says, they can act anywhere, at any time, against anyone... Just imagine for one instant, a hundred people being protected 24/7. That would represent what? Thirty, fifty households? Surveillance of their homes, where they work, where they go for entertainment, schools, residences for seniors? Transportation... No, frankly, that's something that's impossible as well as being completely premature at this point."

I was furious because I knew quite well that he was right. That didn't stop me though.

"So, what's your idea then? Waiting till it's too late? Waiting till there's a victim, something that's foreseeable?"

I could feel my face getting flush with emotion and tears were now welling in my eyes. Jerome put his hand on mine, without saying a word, and squeezed my fingers tightly.

"I'm sorry," Captain Delahousse said. "Of course, I'm going to register your complaint. And ask you to give me a complete list of all your guests, with their names, addresses and phone numbers. But my gut feeling, and I hope it's true, is that this is only a threat — though it is evil and cruel — and it won't have any consequences. Calm down. Take advantage of your honeymoon, go someplace far away. But if you get anything else from the author of these threats, contact me immediately. In that case, we'd consider that there is a clear and imminent danger and deploy our resources. For right now though, just keep your eyes open."

He handed us his card with his direct contact details, including his cell phone number.

"And all my congratulations to the newlyweds, despite this situation," concluded Captain Delahousse, slightly apologetically.

I could tell he wanted to help us, but there wasn't

much he could do right now. I'm sure that he regretted having to speak to us like that and admitting that he had neither the material nor the human resources to help us. But that was the sad reality of a police force constantly faced with drastic budgetary cuts. If only things could have been as simple as they were on TV…

When we left the police station, nothing much had changed for us, and we weren't more reassured than when we came in an hour ago.

We went back home with a knot in our stomachs, dreading the upcoming and uncertain days.

Upon seeing my wedding dress spread out on our bed, I broke down in tears.

CHAPTER 5
A little joke

DELIGHTED TO HAVE HAD SUCH a wonderful evening but exhausted because she'd stayed up much too late, the old lady was slowly making her way down the hall of her senior residence, the metallic end of her cane tapping on the tiles.

"Hello, Suzanne!" a young lady with an authentic smile who worked Sundays at the Genièvres Home welcomed her. "Did you just get back from the afternoon dance?"

"Oh! My beautiful Amelie, you were nearly right there. I was at my grand-daughter's Colombe's wedding, remember? I thought I told you that before I left. It was such a beautiful wedding and reception, and my dear Colombe, if only you could have seen her!"

"Of course! I remember now. You even told me that you wouldn't be spending the night here. Which explains why you just came back now."

"Exactly. And I'm going to go right up to my room and get some rest. I only slept for a couple of hours at one of my niece's, because I wanted to get up early to take part in the 'chamber pot.' Such a fun tradition!"

"Yes, I know it seems like fun, but even though it is a tradition, I don't know if it's one I'd like to have at my own wedding. Speaking of which though, I have to start by finding myself a husband," joked Amelie.

"That is the way it works, but pretty as you are, I'm sure you won't be having any problems for that," the old lady reassured her with a wink.

Then she turned around and faced the young man who had driven her and winked at him too.

"Thanks for driving me here safely, young man. I'm going up to my room and I'll leave you here with this charming young lady."

Suzanne hobbled up to the elevators while smiling at her little joke, one that a caring matchmaker like herself always enjoyed making.

She pushed the button to call one of those large elevators, planned for people in wheelchairs or even medicalized beds. The doors slowly opened with a metallic noise. Suzanne stepped in and went to the back, in front of the mirror as the doors closed behind her. Just before they completely closed, a man's hand blocked them.

The doors squeaked and opened once again, revealing the face of that darn person who was too much in a hurry to wait for the next lift or take the stairs.

"Ma'am! You forgot your purse in the cab."

"Oh! Thank you so much! I'm so tired I wasn't paying any attention."

Suzanne held her free hand out to grab her handbag, but the man quickly pulled it back to himself, surprising the old lady while entering the elevator.

"But..."

The doors closed, imprisoning them both in the metallic cage.

"Please ma'am, I'll bring it to your room, if that's okay with you. With your cane, it's hard."

"Thank you, that's kind of you."

The ascension only took a few seconds, during which time the man observed Suzanne from the corner of his eye, using the back mirror.

The doors reopened.

"What room are you in?" asked the friendly taxi driver.

"Number 213, at the end of the hall."

They walked that way, with Suzanne in front of the young man. When they reached her room, the old lady thanked her makeshift valet once again.

"I'll put it on your desk, don't worry."

"No, that's fine, you've already done so much for me."

"It's not a problem, I like helping people."

Suzanne put her electronic badge in front of the captor and the door opened with a discreet little signal. The chauffeur pushed the door so Suzanne could enter easily and was about to follow her when he heard a voice.

"Excuse me."

A nurse's aide was coming out of the adjoining room.

"Can I help you?" she continued. "Are you looking for someone?"

"Um, no, I was just accompanying my client to her room and helping her carry her stuff inside. I drive a taxi."

"What? I've never seen you around here. For what company? Are you new?"

"I'm freelance, I just arrived in the region, that's why."

Suzanne stuck her head out the door.

"Ah! Marie! How are you? This charming young man has been very obliging. Thank you again."

"A pleasure. Goodbye. Have a nice day then."

He turned around heading for the elevator, but seemingly changed his mind and rushed down the stairs.

Marie came into Suzanne's room with her.

"Suzanne, you should never let anyone into your room. Normally only family members can enter, unless you've authorized someone else. You know the rules."

"You're right, I'm sorry. I was so tired that I left my handbag in the cab, and he said he'd bring it upstairs for me. For once there's a young'un with good manners…"

"You're right, they're now few and far between.

Like in public transportation, when I see all those young people with their headphones on, staring at their phones, who remain seated rather than getting up for someone old, that just revolts me! But anyway. Did you have fun?"

"It was a fantastic wedding. I'm so happy I was able to attend it before I die."

"Suzanne, what are you talking about? You're in good health and you won't be leaving us anytime soon, that's for sure, I forbid that! And you can count on me personally to take care of you and pamper you whenever I can."

"You're so sweet, Marie. I'm going to take a little nap now."

Suzanne could feel that she'd overestimated herself a bit since the day before. She quickly washed her face and took the bobby pins out of her white-haired bun, in which as usual, — because she was still proud of her appearance, — she had placed a ball of white cloth to make it look thicker. She regretted her thick beautiful hair of days gone by and always found it hard to look in the mirror and see her wrinkles.

She was about to pull the green curtain shut on her window when she gazed absent-mindedly outside to the other side of the street where there was an empty building right across from the recent senior residence. It was formerly a textile factory that had gone bankrupt and closed down a couple of years ago and all that was left of it were the concrete walls that were painted over with all sorts of tags and graffiti that only their authors or friends could understand. The city hadn't yet decided to tear it down so it remained standing and because of this, young teens craving alcohol or modern music often squatted it, and Suzanne could even sometimes hear the music in her room, even without her hearing aids.

At other times, there were people who used the building for a place to sleep at night. When the cops didn't have anything else to do they expelled them forcefully. But they always came back as soon as their backs were turned.

Suzanne was holding on to the corner of the curtain, but she suddenly saw some movement in one of the upper floors of the factory. She thought she'd recognized her taxi driver, but from that distance and so surreptitiously, plus taking into account the fact that she was sleeping standing up, the old lady said to herself that it wasn't possible. She had no idea who it could have been.

Confused and totally exhausted, she closed her drapes and went to bed.

CHAPTER 6
A judgment call

I TOSSED and turned all night, sleepless. The same thing was true for Jerome, and I could feel him changing positions all night on his side of our now matrimonial bed.

During the night we both were thinking about the letter.

What should we do now? We had to make a judgment call and couldn't decide on one solution or another.

As the police found themselves unable to materially or humanly help us at this point, we were going to have to take things into our own hands. Face the danger. Except that the worst part was that we weren't playing with a full deck of cards. The author of the letter was alone at the helm, the only skipper on board in his boat of delusions.

What could we do?

Just wait on pins and needles, till there was a new

development? What would that mean? Biding our time, arms crossed, until the announced death occurred?

Or warning all our guests at the wedding, those *potential victims* as they were called in that insane letter?

Would it be better not to let them know about it so they wouldn't be worried or unduly stressed? Like how would Grandma Suzanne react when she learned that she was perhaps targeted by an unbalanced person about whom we ignored everything, including their identity? Would her fragile heart resist such a fright?

That was the worst thing in this case: no one controlled a single thing. Neither the identity of the victim, nor the identity of the guilty party, nor the place, date or method. Nothing at all!

So how could we announce to our friends and family: "*Starting now, and for an indefinite time, make sure you are constantly paying attention, night and day, at home and at your workplace, because someone you don't know may be targeting you... or not... but we can't tell you who, nor when, nor where.*" Tremendous! In other words: how to have paranoia pounding on the doors of the homes of all our dear guests.

How could we alarm ninety-nine people whereas only one seemed to be targeted by that crazy person? At least, if what the letter said was true.

After all, who could affirm that the designated victim wouldn't just be the first one on a long list? Could we believe in the sincerity of a maniac? Maybe that person would like shedding blood and continue their diabolical work with another victim on the list. Then another one, after that one more?

Until all ninety-nine were gone?

"I can't take this anymore," I complained about four in the morning, without having slept a wink. "I'm going to go crazy!"

Jerome snuggled up to my back and put his arms around me.

"We have to try to sleep, or else we'll really go crazy."

But the same questions continued in our minds and the same answers and absences of solutions diabolically bombarded us.

One of them incidentally kept on coming back concerning the author of the letter. I kept referring to that person as "he," maybe because it was easier. But it could also be a woman of course. Nothing in the letter tipped us off about their sex. No grammatical clues. We could have eliminated half of the inhabitants of the planet. A man OR a woman, elementary my dear Watson, wasn't it?

Just the question of whether it was a male or female preoccupied us for about an hour during our sleepless night.

At the break of dawn, physiological and mental exhaustion took the upper hand and Jerome and I finally fell into a type of comatose sleep for a couple of hours.

Unlike the day before, we weren't awakened by a joyful bunch of friends and family members holding their much too realistic chamber pot.

What woke us up that Monday morning was me shouting in my restless sleep.

In less than twenty-four hours, we'd switched from a dream to a nightmare.

CHAPTER 7
Mommy's time

THE VEHICLE PARKED on the side of the sidewalk, with the characteristic noise of an electric motor, and stopped in one of the spots marked with a short time limit.

No one got out, neither on the passenger side nor on the driver's side. No one either rushed up to get in.

The electric motor, though it was running, made no noise, as if it were silently getting ready to pounce just like a tiger.

A little farther down, about three hundred feet or so, other vehicles stopped for an instant, dropping off a kid with their backpack full of books, in the middle of other students whose joyous shouts could be heard between the buildings of the preschool. Strollers rushed from right to left, in which kids still too young for school yawned, their eyes still heavy with sleep, sucking lazily on their pacifiers. Parents ran across babysitters forever in a hurry and teachers who were supervising children running into that inner courtyard protected by iron bars.

An efficient protection against intrusion, but not against voyeurism.

In the electric vehicle, the driver didn't miss a bit of that Monday morning show, one like so many others in a preschool. A frenetic quarter of an hour where parents quickly dropped off their offspring before rushing to work, where grandparents said goodbye to their grandchildren before going to the bakery or to purchase a newspaper or magazine and where the babysitters or nannies chatted for a few minutes between themselves before leaving to take care of the younger kids. Inside, the teachers were getting ready to welcome their little students inside the various classes.

No one thought of anything else rather than their own morning tasks, giving free rein to the individual sitting inside the black electric car. He was looking for young Samuel Coignard.

Little Sam, that cute four-year-old, was ushered into the schoolyard where he found his usual playmates with whom he'd be able to play for ten or fifteen minutes before the bell rang and he'd be locked into the classroom until the next recess.

Sam didn't have any reason to pay attention to that driver who followed him wherever he went. The kid didn't even know he was there. Ah! Kids are so terribly innocent!

Jerome Bastaro's nephew spent his day at school just like all the others, between learning the basics of language, writing and nursery rhymes, with his half an hour recess in the morning, lunch at the canteen right next to his school and his nap in the beginning of the afternoon.

When the bell rang at four, with a smile on his face, he picked up his drawing notebook and crayons, without forgetting his stuffed animal that accompanied him everywhere, and sauntered up to the gate where, according to the day of the week, either his grandpa or grandma would be picking him up.

What little Sam ignored was that the electric car that he saw that morning by the sidewalk would also be there when school let out, idling without any pollutant gases, waiting to pick up one of his classmates. One day it was Kyllian, another Melissa, yet another, Nina.

For Sam, this vehicle was now a part of "Mommy's time," like his teacher Miss Brunnelson always said. He was used to seeing it, as were the other adults. You never pay attention to things you're used to seeing.

But Sam was often jealous of Kyllian, Melissa, and Nina. He would also have liked to ride home in a car like that, which looked like the ones you see in cartoons on TV. But he knew that if he did that, he'd be having his afternoon snack later. And for him, that afternoon snack was sacred, that chocolate croissant or that bowl of cereal with milk and that apple that grandpa had carefully cut into little cubes for him.

But still, when Sam looked at that silent vehicle, with its red and green lights on the roof, the one that started up without making a sound and that disappeared in the one-way street in front of his school, he was a bit jealous.

Yes, Sam would have loved to be driven back home one day in that sparkling black taxi.

MAYBE HIS DREAM would soon come true?

CHAPTER 8
A terrible migraine

AFTER THE LAST guests had helped the newlyweds clean the banquet hall and thanked and congratulated them one last time, everyone realized that the party was finally over.

Two days and one night of joy, fun and shared happiness.

Now it was time to leave and say goodbye.

People were getting ready to go back home, by car, by train or by plane, according to where they lived.

Some lived in the region surrounding Biscarrosse, where the wedding had been held, other departed from that region for cities all over France and even abroad. Guests had come from Belgium, Switzerland, Spain and even from Australia. The Australians would be leaving France in stages, stopping for a day or so to see the maximum number of friends or relatives living in Europe.

Everyone was departing with fantastic memories of

the wedding. Happy to have witnessed Colombe and Jerome's joy and shared it.

Some guests continued their peaceful daily lives as retired people, others were going back to school, high school or university. Most though were simply going back to work, whether it was in a factory, an office, a school, working from home or in the vineyards or fields.

Yet no one could imagine that at this very hour, there was a dark and intangible threat hanging over them.

No one could imagine they were being targeted by an unidentified criminal.

No one could guess that perhaps they had only a few days to live...

AMONGST ALL THOSE HAPPY PEOPLE, that Monday morning Bertrand Signol woke up with the feeling that he hadn't quite recovered from the feasting and drinking during the weekend. He had amply partaken in the before dinner drinks, had enjoyed all the various wines accompanying the dinner and the multiple glasses of champagne that he'd downed during the reception, between dances, songs and games.

He'd awakened with a terrible migraine and a bitter taste in his mouth, probably because of a few too many glasses of champagne. They had assured him that there were no sulfites in it so he wouldn't have a headache in the morning. He was forced to admit that the quantities he'd absorbed must have been the cause. Even before he'd had his morning cup of coffee, he had downed a couple of aspirins. Then he got ready for work. He was an IT developer in a subsidiary of Airbus, and each day he drove from his home in the center of Toulouse to Blagnac, the cradle of the French aeronautics industry.

In his open space office just as spartan as the inside of a rocket, Bertrand spent the entire day writing lines of code to develop the umpteenth software program required for today's aeronautics. A tough task for someone suffering from a migraine after a too festive weekend. He had to make a huge effort to keep his eyes open on his computer screens and took quite a few coffee breaks that morning. Plastic cups were piling up next to all his keyboards.

"You sure look like hell Bertrand," said his colleague Arnie when he saw all the coffee cups. "Tough weekend? You had wild sex all night long or what?"

"Yeah, sure," grumbled Bertrand. "It's not what you think, you old pervert. I was at my cousin Colombe's wedding in Biscarrosse. Had a good time you could say."

"I see. Typical Monday morning hangover... Why don't we go outside for some fresh air?"

"Thanks, but I'm running behind on my work. I gotta finish my first draft of that soft for Wednesday morning to present it to the Executive Board."

"Whatever. I'm going out for a smoke."

"Lazy bum if I ever saw one!" said Bertrand ironically while resuming his frenetic tapping on his keyboards.

The young man, a poster boy for geeks, with his short hair, tortoise-shell glasses, V-necked sweater over a white shirt, souvenirs of adolescent acne, was able to concentrate for a good half an hour before picking up the phone for an internal call.

"Bertrand? It's Carmen, at reception. Am I bothering you?"

"Not at all, what can I do for you?"

"I've got a deliveryman here at the desk who insists on giving you a package. He says you have to sign for it. Can he go up?"

"I'm not expecting anything," said Bertrand, astonished. "Or maybe I just forgot. Sure. Send him up. Thanks, Carmen."

"No problem!"

Three minutes later, an individual walked into the open space with a small package in his hands, without having taken off his motorcycle helmet. He had nonetheless raised his visor, allowing Bertrand to see a pair of dark black eyes topped with bushy eyebrows.

"Bertrand Signol?" asked a deep voice from the helmet.

"That's me."

"Package for you. Can you sign here, please?"

The deliveryman handed a small tablet with a stylet to him.

"Can I see the package before," asked Bertrand. "I can't remember having ordered anything.

The delivery guy nodded, muttering, probably fearing that he'd have to go back because the package had been refused.

Bertrand looked at the package and was astonished that he had no idea who's sent it to him. Sometimes DigitalApps' employees receive small packages, but they were generally accepted by the company at the front desk, and not sent directly to its employees.

What the heck! thought Bertrand as he signed for it.

"Thanks," said the deliveryman leering at him.

He then walked out without even saying goodbye to Bertrand, who remained in front of his screens, not knowing what to do with that unexpected package. Perhaps he'd ordered some IT peripheral equipment or something. Or else, as he sometimes did, he'd asked for a personnel item to be delivered to his workplace, where he often spent more time than in his apartment in Toulouse. Yet he couldn't remember having ordered a thing. But lately he'd been having problems with his memory and concentration, his mind undoubtedly too full of information, codes and private and professional projects. Too full of everything you could say. That was what happened when you continuously lived in a multitasking world! Today's world! The young man was tired after several trying weeks. He hoped he'd soon be able to relax though, as soon as his current project was up and running.

He picked up a letter opener to cut through the tape and ran it around the package before putting it back down in his pencil holder.

Then he opened it and froze when he saw its contents.

"Jesus Christ! What the fuck?" stammered Bertrand, now pallid, quickly closing the package while warily looking around.

CHAPTER 9
An odious letter

TUESDAY MORNING, I woke up after only a couple hours of heavy sleep. The mixture of fatigue and anxiety was getting thicker as each hour went by. When I saw Jerome's drawn face, I understood that his night hadn't been more restorative than mine.

Monday we'd waited the entire day in expectation of some new development concerning that vile threat hanging over our heads and those of our loved ones. Was that threat a real or a fictious one? That was the question running through our minds. We nearly were hoping to have had some news from the author of that odious letter rather than remaining in this terrifying silence. Not knowing had become worse than the opposite. We incidentally and accidentally now understood the true mechanics of terrorism and latent fear. Sensing that something terrible would happen without being able to control a thing. When would it occur? Who would it impact? How would it be carried out? A series of terrifying questions leaving us panting for breath.

"Want me to make you a coffee?" Jerome proposed.

I didn't feel like I could swallow a thing, but like my husband, I felt I really needed some caffeine to cope. We silently drank our hot beverages, snuggled up to one another, incapable of saying anything. Our silence echoed the "terrorist's" silence.

The day went by like that, no news, no enthusiasm from either of us. I looked at my wedding dress on a chair in my bedroom, next to my bedside table, rolled up, thrown there in a movement of wrath. I broke down in tears once again, collapsing on the bed.

"What are we going to do?" I sobbed when Jerome tried in vain to console me. "Who's playing with us like a cat with a mouse? And why?"

I finally conked out in the beginning of the afternoon when my nervous exhaustion won me over.

It was my phone ringing that brought me out of my torpidity. My mother's name was on the screen. I didn't have the strength to answer. She left me a voicemail that I listened to while crying. She said she hoped we were both fine, that she was happy that we were happy. And she asked me what we'd be doing for this week of vacation that had just begun. We both had decided to take the week off to take advantage of our newlywed status. Maybe not the best idea! Had she only known...

But one thing about my mom was that she never

gave up. So as I hadn't answered the first time, she phoned back. Once again I didn't pick up. She phoned again, this time not leaving a message. The third time I answered, her tenacity got the best of me.

"Hi Mom," I whispered with a broken voice.

"Hello, honey. So how are the newlyweds? Happy? Everything you've dreamed of? What are you guys up to? Did you sneak off someplace?"

My mother's logorrhea was unending. Ninon Deschamps, her maiden name Casoli, always asked questions without even waiting for any answers. On the phone she could speak often for many long minutes, you would think she was listening to herself speak and that sufficed. Her many questions finally dried up and I had to force myself to articulate a few words, trying the best I could to hide the tension in my voice.

"Hi Mom. Yeah, we're fine."

"Your voice is scratchy, did you catch cold in your wedding dress? You were so pretty in it, but I already told you that! The most beautiful bride in the world, I hope you know that. Ah! My daughter is now Mrs. Bastaro, she's no longer Miss Dechamps. It seems so strange to think of you like that."

"You know, I'm still Colombe," I said, amused. "I'm still the same person. Your daughter."

"You were such a beautiful bride," Ninon repeated proudly.

"Like all the other brides in the world, don't you agree?"

"Much more! Like your sister was when she got married. I'm not patting myself on the back, but both of you look like your mother, that's what the neighbors always say."

All those fine-sounding words were starting to make me choke up. I was so tired and cranky that I was ready to burst into tears again. I couldn't say anything else.

"You still there?" asked my mom.

"Yeah."

"So, are you guys going anywhere?"

How could I admit that we didn't feel like going anywhere, that we were at the mercy of some crazed fanatic. A crazy person who potentially was targeting *her*, my mother! Her, just like everyone else we were close to. How could I tell her that?

"Colombe?"

Jerome, next to me, was also looking at me pitifully. Inquiring. What was I going to say to my mom?

"No, we don't have anything planned," I managed to get out.

"Really? How come? You should make the most of it! Have fun while you're young!"

Make the most of it? Have fun? We were light years away from stuff like that. But I couldn't decently tell her the whys and wherefores of it.

"I gotta go, Mom. Someone else is calling. Love you. Say hi to dad for me."

I hung up and threw my phone on my bed before my mother could hear my sobs.

. . .

At the end of the afternoon, as usual, Jerome went outside to see if there was anything in the mailbox. This time what horrified us weren't the bills nor the endless flyers.

Amongst the mail we hadn't looked at for at least five days, too busy with all the last-minute preparations for our wedding, we were stupefied to discover an envelope with no names on it, neither ours nor the name of the person who sent it. On the other hand, right in the middle of it there was a symbol that didn't really surprise us, especially after we'd opened it.

It was a simple drawing: it represented two entangled wedding rings, sort of like the rings that magicians try to take apart during their shows. Nothing magical there though! Right above the wedding bands, there was a huge X... As if crossing out or deleting any ideas of felicity.

Then we both gasped when we read the letter.

My dear lovebirds,

Perhaps you thought it was just a little joke I was playing?

I don't think so. You're not stupid enough to think that.

I would imagine, on the contrary, that my first message left you with a bit of bitterness in your stomachs and minds. I'm both apologetic and enchanted!

You think I'm cruel? You haven't seen anything yet... This macabre little game is just beginning.

So, that's all I have to say for right now. This was just a tiny reminder, I don't want you to forget me so quickly, though I certainly don't think that you will.

All this just to tell you to take this little game seriously, for me I'm already laughing my head off!

With all my affection, and... see you soon! Don't lower your guard...

CHAPTER 10
Methodically

UPON FINISHING READING that letter out loud, I was shaking more than someone suffering from Parkinson's.

"This time it's clear," I deplored. "Up till now, we still could believe it was some kind of joke."

"I agree. Short jokes are always the best ones... And if it actually is one, it sure as hell isn't funny!"

The letter was lying on our kitchen island just like a faded autumn leaf.

"What really scares me right now, is to know that the son of a bitch who wrote that came and put it right in our mailbox! It wasn't sent by mail. That means he knows where we live."

"Or maybe he gave it to someone."

"Which would mean the same thing. In either case, he knows where we live. And that makes me even more uncomfortable. What's he gonna do next? Ring our doorbell and hand us a package with a bomb in it?"

Jerome put his hand on mine.

"Let's try and stay calm, I'd imagine that he wants us to be scared out of our minds. Which is the case. Let's try to analyze the elements this letter reveals. Methodically. I'd guess that the author of this stupid letter is a man. Just by the language he's using. What do you think? But for me I'm sure. It's a man. And there are no grammatical mistakes, so someone educated."

I shook my head, dubitative.

"What about a woman who wanted to mask her sex, so we'd be looking for a man? To mix us up even more trying to find the guilty party?"

"That's conceivable of course, but I don't think so. Though this horrible person is having a ball playing with our nerves, I don't see them as a woman pretending to be a man."

"Well, as for me, I'm not that convinced, but I'll keep that possibility in a corner of my brain. Still though, do you realize that they put that letter in our mailbox? Right there, at the end of the sidewalk."

"And they put the first letter in the urn in the banquet hall."

"Reducing the number of persons who could have done it. This time anyone could have dropped it off. Anyone!"

"What about it we asked the neighbors if they didn't see some sleazy person hanging around here?"

"Yeah, sure. The neighbors are all too far away to

have noticed something like that. Plus it doesn't take long to put an envelope into a mailbox. Nothing sleazy about that. Just think of all those people who distribute free papers and flyers. Sometimes they're on foot, or they ride a bike or a scooter. They're quick. People hardly ever notice them. Plus, to make things worse, the person who did that could have disguised themselves as a delivery person, even walking around with a bunch of flyers under an arm with the letter hidden inside."

"Colombe, you never change, do you. You should write screenplays for cop shows!" Jerome joked trying to lighten the atmosphere.

I sighed, forcing myself to calm down. That didn't last long.

"And what if he was disguised as the mailman?"

"You never give up, do you."

"And maybe it was really the mailman?" I insisted, wanted to get to the very end of my line of thought, though it was a twisted one.

Jerome got up from the barstool where he was sitting, and began walking around in circles, just like a caged lion.

"That is exactly what he's trying to do: have us sink into paranoia! Are you listening to yourself Colombe? Now you're making the mailman a suspect! What does that have to do with our urn in the banquet hall? Nothing!"

"Well, anyone could have gone in there," I replied,

defending myself. "And no one is ever afraid of mailmen…"

"You're nuts!"

"What? Just think for one second. A mailman knows a lot about people that he delivers mail to… You could compare him to the paparazzi who go through the garbage cans of famous people. A mailman sees everything he delivers. Packages, letters with the names of senders on them, official mail, registered letters. He knows the name of our banks, our insurance agents. He knows what we read because of the magazines we're subscribed to. He sees if we've gotten fines. He's able to guess when our birthdays are because of cards. And did you ever notice that sometimes you've got envelopes that don't seem closed as well as others? You never wondered if maybe the mailman didn't open a couple of letters before delivering them? Try to take a sneak peek? For example, just imagine a perfumed letter… Maybe the mailman would be curious enough to wonder if you didn't have a mistress!"

"Stop it!" Jerome scolded me. "Please stop, now. All of that is just your imagination. We can't enter his game. We have to keep a cool head, okay? I know it's not easy, but we have to overcome this if we want to prevent him from hurting anyone."

"You're right. But above all, we can't start arguing with each other because of this nutjob. Not right after our wedding! What do you think we should do?"

"I'd say that the first thing would be to go back and

see Captain Delahousse, like he told us to do if we were threatened again."

Which was what we did, bringing him the second letter.

CHAPTER 11
Mentally unbalanced

CAPTAIN DELAHOUSSE WAS JUST as courteous as he was the first time we came to the police station. Yet when Jerome and I went into his office, his face seemed to be quite tense.

"I really didn't think I'd be seeing you again," said the policeman, inviting us to sit down. "So that first letter wasn't just some sort of sick joke then because now there's another one, if my colleague at the front desk was correct."

I had the second letter that we'd received just a couple of hours ago in my hand and gave it to him.

"As you can see, this crazy bastard hasn't finished harassing us with his threats."

The cop took time to read through that anonymous letter, while chewing gum, probably to mask his frustration.

"That seems clear to me," he said apologetically. "We're looking at some mentally unbalanced person here. But still, these are just threats and not acts."

I could feel that Jerome wasn't going to like Delahousse's conclusion. He exploded.

"What? You're getting ready to tell us that you're going to remain arms crossed and do nothing, waiting until this nutjob actually does something? That would be too late, and we'd be crying over the death of one of our loved ones. Because that's what this is all about: killing someone we know, someone we're close to!"

The captain sighed, leaned towards us, his elbows on his desk, his hands joined together below his chin. It was evident that he was trying to find the right words to appease us. Of course, that was his role, he was torn between the desire to help us and the legal resources he had available.

"Do you understand that threats like these, whether they're verbal or written, aren't a crime?"

Neither of us replied to that purely theoretical question of his, and he continued.

"Even though threats do contain, just like this one, a clear intention to commit a crime. In French legislation, if there is no act, there's no crime, it's unfortunately just as simple as that."

"So you're not going to do anything then? You'll remain entrenched in your position, armed with your sacrosanct laws, until one of the people we know is killed? Tell me then Captain, when that happens, should we contact you by email, a letter, or call you?" I exploded, furious.

"Mrs. Bastaro, believe me, I understand how angry you are. And I never said that we weren't going to do anything to try to get to the bottom of this case. On the contrary, with this second letter, we know that the author is serious, and I'll be able to react, try to get the ball rolling. Yesterday I invited you to file a complaint, but now I can open an investigation and I'll be able to engage more important resources."

"Such as?" asked Jerome. "Having our ninety-nine loved ones watched by your colleagues?"

Delahousse shook his head.

"Unfortunately I still don't have the resources for that. But though we can't identify the victim this unbalanced person is targeting, we can try to find the author of these threats. So what I can do now is to ask for scientific analyses of both of these letters. Even if I don't think we'll find much, as both of you have already manipulated them, I imagine. Who knows, maybe the author will have left some fingerprints on the paper or the envelope… If luck is on our side, those fingerprints could correspond to one of the persons in the AFIS."

"The AFIS?"

"Yes, the Automated Fingerprints Identification System, AFIS. Of course, to get a hit, the author of those letters would have had to have some type of criminal record. If that's not the case, he won't be registered in our nationwide database, and we won't be able to identify him. But that is something we now can do as for the moment, we don't have any other leads. What do you think?"

Jerome and I looked at each other, both of us stressed. We finally had an ounce of hope, we certainly wanted to exploit it.

"We don't have any better options, so let's go for it, of course," replied my hubby for both of us.

"Perfect. In that case, I'm going to open an investigation and register this evidence before sending it to Toulouse."

"Toulouse? Why so far?"

"It's the closest FL around here."

"If you could avoid using abbreviations and acronyms Captain, it would be easier for us to understand."

"Excuse me. That's one of the five French Forensic Laboratories that are accredited to do analyses of fingerprints on this type of evidence. The only downside is the turnaround time. They've got a lot to do, as I'm sure you can imagine. Their services cover various domains such as ballistics, physics, chemistry, biology, toxicology, drugs, explosives, fake documents, and other things like that. I don't want to give you any false hopes, you'll have to be patient."

I sighed noisily. The captain was taking us on a roller coaster ride, blowing hot then cold, disillusions after hope.

"We're back to square one then: waiting," I deplored.

"I'm sorry. In this case, though it's cruel to say,

neither of us has very many cards in our hands. The author of those threats is the one who's dealing. So until you know more, you're going to have to keep your eyes peeled and pay attention. If I follow his logic, he's not going to act soon. He wants to play with you, that's evident, he's talking about a challenge, he wants to test you. How? Got me. But I'm sure he'll recontact you in some way soon."

Captain Delahousse's last words seemed like a horrible harbinger to us. We would have given anything for this not to have been true and have this nightmare end. I prayed to myself that the policeman was wrong, that the nutjob who was sending us these letters would abandon his macabre project. But we had to face the facts, we'd never be at peace with that terrifying sword of Damocles hanging right over both our heads, the heads of our loved ones, the heads of those ninety-nine guests at our wedding.

And one of them in particular.

But which one?

CHAPTER 12
An unhealthy look

Summer 2008

THE YOUNG TEEN WAS UNCOMFORTABLE, *distraught. Each time she left home to go to the gym she was being watched. That was where, between those four gray concrete walls and that ceiling made from corrugated iron sheeting where you suffocated in summer and froze in winter, she was able to pursue her passion. That leotard, a thin layer of sequined fabric, stuck to her moist skin during gymnastics competitions in June, but didn't prevent her from shivering in February. Moreover, it barely covered her butt and stuck to the budding forms of that complexed teen, one having problems with her changing and erratic anatomy, something that made her uneasy.*

But she loved performing on the beam, on the vault, or doing flips, jumping, doing splits and bridges so much that once she was on the ground or using the uneven bars, she forgot the surrounding world. Those two hours of gym, twice a week, were an outlet for the rest of the week, one where she went to school, did her homework, phoned her friends, or secretly had a crush on some boy.

Except for one thing: to walk to the gym, she had to go through a neighborhood she hated. Not that it was actually one of ill repute, but because of one person who lived in one of the apartments there, a guy she couldn't stand. You could say that he was her pet peeve, her scourge, her parasite. She'd politely told him several times to back off, but he kept on coming back, that idiot! It's true that boys often lag behind girls to reach puberty and maturity, during that difficult age where both sexes are still trying to find who they are, trying to attract the opposite sex. But that guy, with his ugly pimple face and dandruff in his hair and on his shoulders, there was no way that she could ever be attracted by him!

The worst thing was when he came into the gym during the last half hour of training for the youngest group, of which she was a part. With the fallacious pretext of basketball training, as the gym was multipurpose and compartmentalized, he tried lamely to shoot a few baskets, mostly missing, while taking advantage of the location to ogle her leotards in movement. She could feel his dirty look on the top of her legs and her butt when she spread her legs and did cartwheels. Plus she could only too well imagine his eyes salaciously zooming in on her breasts that were accentuated by the spandex, or on her toned buttocks that the cloth only covered halfway.

Sometimes that even made her lose her concentration

and she had to try two or three times before succeeding in what she was doing. She could have killed him for spoiling her life like that!

Then when the gym class was over, she would run into the changing rooms and upon exiting, the muffled bounces or the orange basketball had disappeared.

Not for long though.

It was even worse when she was walking back home. On the way there, it was still light outside.

Whereas on the way back home...

She would begin with her girlfriends from gym but had to finish alone.

That was where he hid in the shadows to wait for her.

And there was no other itinerary than taking that poorly lit street.

That was where he'd appear, when she was the least expecting it, with his sickly, slimy smile plastered in the middle of his ravaged face, with craters in it like the plains in Verdun in 1916!

"Hi," he'd say with this twangy voice.

"Leave me alone," she'd immediately reply. "You still don't get it? I can't stand the sight of you, dammit! Move it!"

Yet he remained in front of her, taller than she was by a head. She tried to move around him. He held his hands out to her. She pushed him away with contempt.

"Just once," he'd continue.

"Not even in your dreams. Have you looked at yourself in the mirror? Plus, even if I did like you, you

know that it's impossible between us. Go away. Let me past."

He would clench his fists in frustration, biting his lip nearly until it bled and would finally decide to leave, pulling on the crotch of his slacks, embarrassed by an uncontrollable erection each time he got near her.

She finally could go back home to her parent's house, calm down in a hot shower, though already dreading her next gym session.

CHAPTER 13
The final curtain

THAT TUESDAY MORNING, at the break of dawn, right as the sun was just beginning to rise in the East, Suzanne woke up with a jolt, as if she'd had a horrible nightmare.

Her unkempt white hair was sticking to her nape, on the pillow. Her heart was pounding, as if the nightmare was continuing — chasing after her — after she'd awakened. The old lady couldn't remember having slept so poorly in ages. Actually though as she'd aged, little by little her dreams seemed to have vanished, as if her memory was now retired too, her subconscious already dead, much before her body which persisted in enduring despite the wear and tear of her old age. An interminable life!

Yet Suzanne frequently knew that one day or another her hourglass would be empty, the same thing was true for everyone. But how? When? Those were the type of thoughts that often ran through the old lady's head. Some mornings she would wake up with a vague impression that the new day would be the last one she'd cross out on her calendar.

But that Tuesday, after having woken up with a cold sweat on her body, Suzanne feared that this would actually be the case.

She had vague images in her mind, stemming from her recent nightmare. She saw herself as a beautiful young lady, a long, long time ago. Someone from a respected middle-class family, someone who mothers must have seen as a good "catch" for their sons. But someone who never had anything to reproach. Why all those distant memories? Why had she woken up suddenly afraid?

Suddenly, still lying down in her bed, her eyes only half open, a hand on her heart, trying to calm its disorderly beating, Suzanne thought she heard the characteristic squeaking of her door opening.

Was Marie already bringing her breakfast? That's strange, Suzanne thought, *they usually don't bring it until eight thirty.* Glancing at her alarm clock with its red numbers, the old lady saw that it was only six o'clock. Yet, and she'd bet her life on it, she was sure that she saw the door opening slowly out of the corner of her eye.

She squinted a few instants to adapt her eyes to the subdued light in her room. Her pupils dilated slowly. That was when, on her right, she thought she saw a silhouette moving like a silent shadow. She thought she saw shoes that were sliding, almost floating rather than walking, on the linoleum in her room. She didn't recognize the Crocs that the personnel usually wore.

Was someone else other than Marie approaching her bed, she wondered.

Suzanne wanted to say something, but words didn't come out of her mouth.

The shadow was now close to her. Now that it was just a few inches from the bed, the old lady knew that it was a man.

She slowly turned her head and thought she recognized him. Though she couldn't remember who he was, she at least thought she'd run across him someplace but couldn't remember where nor when.

But it was something that happened not too long ago.

The shadow leaned over the bed, his eyes shining in the darkness of the room.

Now Suzanne could distinguish his features more clearly and a light came on in her brain.

Ah! You again? What are you doing here? she wanted to know, but those words were fettered in her mouth that the man's powerful hand had just closed.

The old lady opened her eyes wide, first of all because she was surprised, and then because she was being asphyxiated. His wide palm was covering her lips and her nose, making it impossible for her to breathe. A muted pressure invaded her chest cavity, immediately followed by a sharp pain in the top of her back and then along her left arm.

What do you...? she tried to understand. *Why are you here now? I paid you the other day!*

Suzanne's poor oxygen-deprived brain thought she recognized the features of that young man who had brought her back, two days ago, in his taxi after her grand-daughter's wedding.

Each second the pain was harsher, unbearable. A cold sweat covered her thin body while the last erratic beats of her heart pounded in her ears.

Suzanne's brain, quickly fading now, could imagine the insanely reddened eyes staring at her from above.

A last powerful and painful twinge tightened her heart. A tightness like she'd never before felt in her entire existence.

The last tightening of the vice of life was fleeing.

∽

WHEN MARIE CAME in with Suzanne's breakfast tray two hours later, the nurse's aide nearly dropped it when she saw the old lady's characteristic posture and her glassy eyes. Though it wasn't the first time, you never could get used to seeing one of your residents' dead bodies. She knew that this would be the case for everyone, that one day or another it would be the final curtain for them, and they'd leave to make room for a new resident, after their personal belongings had been moved out and the room had been cleaned and disinfected. That was the sad reality for a senior citizens' home: empty rooms didn't bring in any money.

Yet when she saw Suzanne's frozen features that morning, Maria was overwhelmed. Most of the time, when residents passed in their sleep, their faces were serene and peaceful. Suzanne though seemed to have passed while screaming, her open mouth as proof of her last silent cry.

Marie informed the doctor on-call who came as quickly as possible.

"Just to think that last weekend she was partying at a wedding," Marie said when he arrived.

"What can I say Marie, that's life. One day you're dancing, the next day you're dead. Life is like a huge Ferris wheel in an amusement park: you get in, you go around, and then you get off. And then someone else takes your place," the doctor said philosophically.

News rapidly ran through the grapevine in the halls, upstairs and in the pavilions, while the doctor was making his diagnostic.

"This dear Suzanne undoubtedly died from a myocardial infarction. A heart attack, to put it simply. Nothing exceptional at her age, unfortunately. A quick death, while she was sleeping, much better than some painful condition that never seems to end, don't you agree?"

He filled out the death certificate noting that as the cause of death and asked the director to inform her family of the eighty-eight-year-old lady's passing.

CHAPTER 14
Syllogisms

HOW COULD I have told her that it seemed much, much worse than anything she could have imagined when my mother called me.

"Colombe, I've got terrible news for you honey! Your grandma just died."

I received that news just as if someone had socked me in the plexus and cut my air supply off. If only my mother could have seen the twists and turns that occurred in my brain in those few seconds when I tried to assimilate Grandma Suzanne's death!

I had time to say to myself that the psychopath who had been harassing us for the past three days had struck, in line with his promise to do away with one of the ninety-nine guests at our wedding. Then I thought how easy it was, but how cowardly it was also to kill a poor defenseless old lady.

Sitting on the beach at Lake Biscarrosse where Jerome and I had gone for some peace and quiet, I looked out to the center of the body of water. I must have been cogitating for quite a few seconds when I heard my mother's voice on the phone again.

"Colombe?" Did you hear me? Your Grandma Suzanne is dead."

"Oh no, good Lord, yes I heard you, I'm in shock. That's terrible," I stammered, my heart broken. "What happened?"

But I didn't want to know!

"The doctors said she had a heart attack. At her age, she was pushing ninety you know, it's something that's not rare, though it was sudden. Life is terrible, you know. Just a couple of days ago we were all having fun together and now I'm going to have to take care of my mom's funeral," she said, choking back a sob.

Deep down inside I had a feeling that happiness would be followed by heartache. The warning Jerome and I had received was clear.

"Do you want me to help you with the paperwork, Mom?"

"That's nice of you, but don't worry. Your grandmother had already anticipated her passing and made her last wishes known. Everything is already taken care of in her will and at the funeral home. I just have to validate all that. Oh! It's horrible to have to sum up a whole life by signing a couple of papers," my mother lamented. "Don't worry though, I've got this. And you've got much better things to do, my beautiful newlywed."

Better things to do? I thought to myself, letting the

sand slide through my hand I'd shaped as a funnel. I wasn't so sure.

After everything that had just occurred, I couldn't rule out the existence of a cause-and-effect relationship between the threats given by that unknown person and my grandmother's sudden death. Undoubtedly the fruit of my overflowing imagination, which was what I was hoping with my heart and soul, as the opposite would have terminated all my illusions.

I broke down in tears with a lump in my throat. My mother, at the other end of the line, tried to calm my heartache, inviting me to remember the best moments I'd shared with my grandmother.

"You have to remember how beautiful and how good your Grandma Suzanne was. A genuinely nice person, you know that just as well as I do."

"Yes, you're right," I replied between two sobs.

Jerome, next to me, had his arm around my shoulders, and delicately kissed my hair. I was able to calm down a bit.

"When will the funeral be?"

"The day after tomorrow, at Parentis Cemetery. You don't have to come, dear. My mom wouldn't have wanted to spoil your wedding."

"You're joking! Of course I'll come to accompany grandma to the very end. Because I love her."

We spoke for another couple of minutes about this and that and urged each other to remain strong. When I hung up, I burst into tears in Jerome's arms.

"I can't believe that this was just a horrible coincidence! She was fine the whole weekend! You could tell she was overjoyed, and she looked great!"

"Yup, and Napoleon, fifteen minutes before he died, was still alive! You're heard of La Palisse…"

"Stop that! How can you joke in a moment like this? You're crazy."

"I just want you to understand that I love your grandma, but at her age, lots of people die from heart attacks or just because of old age."

I knew deep down inside that he was right, but I continued, wanting to reach the end of my logical reasoning.

"You've heard of syllogisms, right? Well here's one. A crazy guy says he's gonna kill one of the ninety-nine guests at our wedding, AND Grandma Suzanne was at our wedding AND she just died. THEREFORE my grandmother was potentially one of the guests he targeted."

"Stop! You're delusional, that's paranoia. And we can't allow ourselves to be paranoiac!"

I quickly got up, without even brushing off the sand on my shorts.

"Dammit Jerome! How can I prevent myself from thinking like that? And how the hell can you suddenly be so calm?"

I was furious and walked off to the shore where a few sad little waves were coming in. I could hear my hubby walking towards me, trying to calm me.

"I'm sorry darling. I understand what you must be

feeling, and I feel the same way. But let's not fight about it. We have to face this together."

He put his arm around my waist, on my left, and we both looked out towards the middle of the lake, at someone paddling across it.

"We have to inform Captain Delahousse," I told him.

"He's got other fish to fry than to take care of a granny who died from a heart attack in an old people's home, don't you think?"

"Not just any granny, Jerome! Mine! Who was a guest at our wedding a couple of days ago, meaning..."

He cut me off, saying he knew. The syllogism...

"We have to tell him. He'll do what he wants with that info, but at least he'll be informed. I'm calling him as soon as we get back."

Half an hour later, when I hung up from my phone call with the captain, I felt even worse than before, because of what he'd told me.

CHAPTER 15
Intimate convictions

IT WAS SUPPOSED to be a nice evening, at least for the temperature outside, the exact opposite of my soul, cooled down once again by what Captain Delahousse had told me. I was sitting outside on our patio, facing the rows of maritime pines that led to our house, when he answered the phone.

"Ah! Mrs. Bastaro, I was getting ready to call you. But unfortunately not to give you any good news."

"After all I've been through that's not going to make much of a difference. But go ahead."

"So here's the thing. I finally got my colleagues in Toulouse to analyze your documents, and I've got the results in front of me. I would have like to tell you that we have a lead, even a minute one, but..."

"But what?" though it seemed to me I already knew the answer.

"But they didn't come up with anything. Except

for your fingerprints, yours and your husband's, as well as mine, they didn't find any others. So we're back to square one I'm afraid. Your mysterious letter writer is still as mysterious! I'm sorry about this, I would have liked them to find something, but it would seem that your guy is no dunce. Or at least he's someone who was very careful. Using anonymous letters, completely ordinary paper and envelopes, leaving no fingerprints, he's taking all his precautions. No doubt about it, he likes to play, and he likes to have all his cards in his hand. All we can do is wait until he pulls out his next trump."

The policeman's metaphors didn't affect me, though I continued with them.

"I'm afraid that" — and this really hit home — "that he already showed his cards, Captain. And now I'm just hoping he doesn't have an ace up his sleeve… and that this nightmare is over."

"What do you mean by that? Did you receive another letter? He turned his words into action?"

I sighed, undecided on how to reveal my doubts.

"I'm not sure of anything, but I have like an ominous intuition."

Then I told the policeman how I'd just learned that my grandmother had passed away and why I thought that perhaps it was caused by that nutjob who was terrorizing us. On the other end of the line, while explaining my theory, I could hear the captain saying *hum, okay, ah, I see,* things like that. When I finished and had asked the policeman if he could open an investigation on the death of someone close to me, I was nearly sure of what he would reply.

"Mrs. Bastaro, from what you just told me, your grandmother's death seems like totally normal and natural to me. Plus that was what the medical certificate stated."

I wanted to insult his cowardice but stopped myself. Had I been face to face with him, my angry eyes would have undoubtedly sufficed to undermine his certainties. I let him continue.

"I do understand that you could see this as a deliberate act, rather than just an unfortunate coincidence. Does the death certificate mention anything like traces of blows, a fight, black and blue marks, anything like that? If we don't have any proof, for me it's just a death, a sad one obviously, but something natural. You can't see evil everywhere."

"That is incredible!" I shouted out, furious now. "He wrote: *I won't be telling you WHO nor WHEN nor HOW…* Maybe you already forgot? That means he could kill anyone, at anytime and anywhere! So excuse my mood here, but yes, I think I've got the right to see evil everywhere!"

I could hear his chair squeaking in the phone. The captain must have gotten up.

"Okay. Maybe you are right. I'll send some men over to your grandmother's residence. It's not very far and that will help us get to the bottom of this case. I'll inform you as soon as we know more. And in the meanwhile, you two, you and your husband, be careful and send me the list of the guests at your wedding, like I asked you to. Maybe that will give us some ideas on how to continue the investigation."

CHAPTER 16
Agoraphobia

IT WAS impossible for us to remain at home without going outside. If push came to shove, we could have had our food delivered, but neither Jerome nor I wanted to plunge into endless gloom and doom. So we left our house for an outing that nonetheless seemed strange to us, as for the past three days all we'd thought about were ourselves: we went shopping.

The only time we'd left our home was to go see Captain Delahousse, followed by a short moment on the lakefront. We were both inhabited by some sort of intangible fear, totally ignoring what to fear, as well as who to fear. Though we didn't feel we were personally targeted, we still were the prey of that infernal conspiracy.

When Jerome parked the car in the lot that was about three-quarters full, I couldn't stop myself from peering out into each car we drove in front of, whether they were empty or full, such as that taxi that was parked right in front of the entrance and whose motor was idling. What had I been expecting to be honest with you? That I'd calmly discover someone wearing a cap and sunglasses sitting behind his steering wheel and that he'd be that unsub who had been harassing us? But I didn't know a thing about him! Nothing at all!

Yet I felt that he must have been near us as he'd already delivered two messages right to our home.

FOR THE ENTIRE time we spent in the supermarket and surrounding stores, I felt a type of agoraphobia that I'd never experienced in my life. How many other phobias would I be developing because of that latent apprehension and anxiety? Fear of receiving mail? Fear of having someone close to me die? Fear of being continuously watched, spied upon? Maybe those fears didn't even have names. I couldn't have cared less, though.

We did our shopping as quickly as possible. We barely even spoke to one another. We'd drawn up a short shopping list before leaving and rushed down the aisles. Each time we arrived at an end cap, we looked up and down the next aisle to see who already was there. The supermarket seemed to be a labyrinth filled with dangers in each section, uncertainty in each aisle, and dead ends where we didn't want to get stuck in.

I felt like I was smothering.

"Let's get the hell out of this place," I said, out of breath, my head pounding.

I FELT BETTER AS SOON as we were outside in the parking lot, less oppressed, but still just as worried.

I was holding the bar of the shopping cart, just like a sailor in the middle of a storm, afraid I'd fall, afraid my legs would give out under me. My entire body showed completely understandable signs of weakness. We had hardly slept for four days now. A couple of hours here, a couple there, not enough to feel rested.

When I was just a few feet away from our car, I suddenly jumped.

"Oh no! That can't be true!"

"What?" asked Jerome, worried.

I moved my chin towards the car.

"The windshield."

I was afraid to advance, just as if the shopping cart had brakes on it.

"It's nothing," Jerome who continued to advance tried to reassure me.

I followed him, slowly pushing the shopping cart.

I saw him walk up to the car, lean over to the middle of the windshield and reach for the windshield wipers, on the driver's side, below which a piece of white paper was stuck.

I was petrified, I didn't want to watch, I was going crazy with all those horrible messages. Had that psychopath followed us to the store, waited until we went in, and then put an additional warning on our car?

My tired brain was exhausting itself with so many crazy questions while Jerome was reaching for the paper, turning it over, and... and bursting into a nervous laugh when he read it.

"Don't panic," he replied between two spasms. "It's just an ad for a traveling circus that's going to perform in Biscarrosse Square."

I sighed, relieved, but at the same time began to cry. I felt like I was going to have a nervous breakdown, too much was too much.

We put our shopping into the trunk of the car and drove back home.

However, once we'd arrived and put the groceries away, I opened my purse and realized that our house was far from being a safe haven, a more intangible danger was still lurking around it.

The email I opened on my phone proved that.

CHAPTER 17
A regrettable coincidence

WHEN I READ THE "IDENTITY" of the email sender, it was as if someone had stabbed me in the back.

From: Anonymousemail

"Shit!"

That was exactly what I felt at that exact second. I already knew I'd hate the content of that message.

And that was absolutely true, especially as the way he had started out.

My dear happy newlyweds...

. . .

No doubt whatsoever, this time it wasn't some dumb flyer for a traveling circus, rather our own personal circus that had premiered last Sunday.

"Something wrong?" asked Jerome when he saw how pale I was.

"Wrong isn't strong enough," I replied, holding up my phone between us so we both could read at the same time. "You didn't get anything?"

He took his phone out of his pocket. Then sighed.

"I think I got exactly the same thing."

This is how the message began:

Before getting down to business, I want to be both polite and delicate. Yes, I'm capable of that too, you can be sure of it.

I'd like to say how sorry I am for your loss.

Why? Nowadays, news flies. We live in a hyperconnected world where everyone knows everything, where there are no secrets and where things are shared by a simple snap of your fingers!

Really, I share the heartache you must have — Jerome, and especially you, Colombe — ever since that unfortunate passing of Grandma Suzanne.

"That scumbag! Son of a bitch!" I shouted, completely worked up. "See, my grandma didn't just die because it was her time! He's confessing!"

"Wait a second, that's not really clear," replied Jerome. "Let's keep on reading."

I can already hear you screaming and damning me, aren't you? You must be accusing me of having been the one who was at the origin of that humble old lady's passing. Oh come on! Let's be serious, just for once. Did you really think that our little game could be over so quickly? When we were just starting to have fun together?

"That bastard is the only one having fun," I said bitterly.

So let me be clear, writing in black letters on your white screen: I have absolutely nothing to do with Grandma Suzanne's death. Let's just say it was a regrettable coincidence, and I do understand you here, that perhaps confused you, made it think it was me. So, if it's fine with you, let's just say this subject is finished and go on to the next one, the more interesting one in my opinion.

Let's talk about the method, alright?

I imagine that you have been doing your utmost to try to identify me. And you're probably thinking that you'll quickly be able to put an end to this thorn in your feet. That would be the best way, to attack it at the roots, cut down that rotten tree before it infects all the others around it with its mental illness.

I don't want to disappoint you, but if you do that, you'll be heading straight into a wall of incomprehension, a dead end, an inextricable enigma. I don't have the pretension of being impossible to find, but I'm proud to think that trying to catch me would be just as hard as trying to bare-handedly catch an eel, if you understand that image.

Let me be a good sport: I'll give you a helping hand. Aren't I generous? Rather than trying to figure out who I am, why don't you try to discover my motives?

That way perhaps, instead of identifying the author, you could try to find out who will be the victim... and why!

Sometimes all you have to do is to think outside the box. Look on the other side of the mirror. Step back to better encompass the big picture. Well, I'm sure you understand what I'm getting at.

I don't want to monopolize too much of your precious time. You've got other fish to fry rather than reading my email!

Before slipping away like a shadow, and to warm your hearts and lift your spirits, I wrote this little poem just for you, straight from my soul.

Here it is.

"This nutcase is Machiavellian!" shouted

Jerome. "If he thinks he's gonna appease us with a poem, that's worse than disgusting."

"We still have to read it."

The most beautiful thing on earth

The most beautiful thing on earth
Tell me, it must be
The love you have for others.
That powerful feeling
Can actually sooth
And become a solution, that
Is swept away
By such a lovely impetus.
Letting your heart speak,
That incredible organ
Where are hidden many closer
Feelings inside...
You must always dare
Tell your loved ones
Much sooner rather than later,
Before you see the Grim Reaper,
That horrible harpy,
Who actually only comes once.
Because though you don't like it,
People may say
They'll escape from its scythe...
When that day comes,

Often by surprise, and
Believe it, that day will come,
For each and everyone!

I WINCED when I finished reading that so-called poem that started out by talking about love and that finished with a poorly disguised threat, just like a symbol of what was happening to us: after our wedding, the threat of an anonymous death.

The email ended with two more sentences:

So MY LITTLE LOVEBIRDS, did you like this poem?
I wrote it just for you my dears!

CHAPTER 18
Foxy lady

Summer 2008

IT'S *summer and at the riverside, its water is flowing languidly with a delicate shivering in your ears. The past days had been suffocating and sweltering, even at night the temperature never fell below 75°. Meaning that group of teens really wanted and needed to cool off in that nearby cool river.*

Summer vacation had gone by too slowly for those who couldn't go someplace with their families or who preferred to meet up with friends in their village out in the hicks. Finally, a foosball and a pinball machine at the local Café, a welcoming river during the days with banks that were ideal for barbeques and bonfires at night, not forgetting of course a few six-packs and S'mores, with some good music and friends to kill time, were sufficient to make those teens happy.

Nearly all of them.

Because outside of the steaming mercury, their overheated hormones also played a part in that electric atmosphere that summer. Just fifteen years old for some of them, sixteen for others, ages that were tormented by exacerbated or repressed desires, depending.

A few of them were already boasting an assumed eroticism whereas others were painstakingly occulting their attributes they dreamed of eliminating. But on that riverbank, it was hard to remain bundled up in a big towel, looking at the others frolic in the current, laughing, splashing each other, screaming, briefly and secretly looking at the opposite sex out of the corners of their eyes with amused jibes.

Teens in all their splendor!
All their ambiguities!
All their black horrors too, sometimes.

"Come on in swimming with us, don't just sit there! The water's nice and warm!"

"Who's nice and warm?" immediately replied a masculine voice followed by raucous laughter.

"Your old lady!"

"What do you know about my mother, you asshole?"

"I already had her at the end of my dick!"

Nothing more was needed to trigger a friendly aquatic battle, splashing each other, trying to dunk the others, disorderly fun. Enough noise so that the teenager, now nearly a young lady, was forgotten on the bank, sweating in her towel. An ideal cocoon to hide her budding figure, one she was ashamed of, one she didn't seem to fit into, though her best friend told her she was a "real foxy lady!" But a fox that was afraid to be hunted down!

There suddenly was a shadow hovering over her while she had lowered her head to look at the book she'd been trying to get into for days without succeeding. A shadow with bulging muscles, with hair like Patrick Swayze, eighties style peroxidized curls, emerging from the water just like in Point Break.

"You're like a cat," said that shadow with a charming smile, "are you afraid of water?"

She slowly raised her head. She didn't want him to imagine that she couldn't wait to look him in the eye. She was too afraid that he would realize how stirred she was, that he'd remark how her lips twitched when she spoke to him, the goosebumps on her epidermis when she was close to that Adonis.

"Ah no..." she finally stammered.

"What's the problem then? You don't know how to swim? You're on the rag?"

"Don't be so crude!"

But visibly the young girl's snubs didn't affect him. To tease her a bit more, he shook his wet hair just like a wet dog would.

"Don't be so dumb, dammit!" she shouted slapping him on his calves, something that didn't cause him to move.

Quite the opposite, he sat down next to her laughing.

"You don't have a sense of humor! Just relax! You

want a massage?" he asked, putting his two hands on the young girl's shoulders.

She felt an uncontrollable shiver wind down her backbone. She tried to get away from his hold, but with no real conviction; her body betraying her.

"No, I'm fine, why don't you go back in the water."

Now the boy's hands were tactfully brushing over her clavicles. She lowered her head and closed her eyes, abandoning herself with a muffled sigh.

"There you go, just let me do my thing, you beautiful mermaid who doesn't like the water. Wow, are you ever tense, I can tell. What's wrong?"

"Nothing, I'm fine, don't worry."

"It's nice here, isn't it? We're on vacation, it's hot out, we're all having fun, and there's a good-looking guy who's taking care of you…"

"That's enough, I think you're getting too big for your britches," the young lady said ironically.

"You're totally right there… Wanna take a peak?"

"No thanks! I already saw plenty of ugly stuff."

"You don't know what you're missing."

"Honest to God, you're crazy! Are you actually listening to yourself? You know that between you and me it's Mission Impossible, *even if you think you're Tom Cruise."*

"You're right, that's what's driving me crazy… crazy about you!"

His fingers on her tight shoulders… A delicate moment she forced herself to put an end to now, with a firm yet gentle gesture.

"Stop that, please. You can see they're talking about us."

And it was true that thirty or so feet down, the others were no longer horsing around and were looking out from the corners of their eyes at that improbable couple on that little pebble-covered beach. Complicit smiles were exchanged, while others had envious smirks.

One of them in particular caught the attention of that young girl and her much too handsome massager.

"You're right," confirmed the young man with his peroxidized blond hair, "I've got the impression that everyone doesn't like what I'm doing... But what the hell!" he laughed. "Him and me we're not playing in the same league, don't you agree?"

"Cuz you think you're good-looking?"

"Not only do I think so, but when I look in your eyes, you do too... and in theirs," he said motioning with his chin to the gaggle of girls in the lake.

Apart from that jabbering group, there was a boy sitting on the other shore, on top of one of the rocks overlooking the lake. He was sitting, his arms around his legs, looking down angrily at them. Could his eyes have shot arrows, he certainly would have aimed one of them right at that tall blond guy in the tight black trunks. Between the two of them, things had always been tense, as if nourished by some vague rivalry, one that was actually unwarranted. But as the famous French author Blaise Pascal wrote: "The heart has its reasons, of which reason knows nothing."

And how could you be reasonable when nearly every

day you run across a creature who ignores that she'd been molded from the same clay as goddesses?

"You know what?" the girl said, suddenly getting up. "Quit showing off, you're too dumb!"

She threw her towel into her bag and took her skirt and top out of it, putting them on as fast as she could before walking away from the water.

No one dared to follow her as her silhouette disappeared behind that bridge over the river.

CHAPTER 19
The hearse

AS SOON AS I'd finished reading that anonymous email the night before, I transferred it to Captain Delahousse. Hoping that the police force would be savvy enough to crack its origins. I undoubtedly was influenced by all the crime shows on TV, in which criminal cases were solved thanks to technological expertise that investigators had, becoming cyber-investigators. But in real life, was that really the way things happened?

Wednesday was going to be a complicated day, weighed down by an event we would have preferred not to attend: the funeral services of my Grandma Suzanne, which would be taking place in the afternoon in Sanguinet, the town where she was born.

I cried all morning and that even got worse when I had to decide what to wear for her funeral. How could I put on black clothing without thinking of the white dress I'd worn only four days ago?

Jerome had tried in vain to appease me, telling me

that life was but a wheel that you couldn't stop, that some people died on their birthdays, others going to their own weddings, others on Christmas day, but his words didn't console me.

When we arrived at the church, we saw my parents, and my mom's red eyes welcomed me before her arms wrapped me in a powerful maternal hug. I let myself go just like a little girl and burst into tears.

"Sweetie," my mom murmured. "This is so awful! It was so quick!"

Right then I didn't have enough strength to tell her what else, excepting Grandma Suzanne's death, was bothering us.

"We're going to miss her so much."

Other members of the family came up to greet us, including my cousins Bertrand and Pascal, then Monique, one of my grandmother's sisters, and Robert, her husband. Besides those family members, there were a handful of people I didn't recognize standing outside of the church. Seeing how most of them were gray-haired and quite elderly, I assumed that they were probably also residents of the old people's home where Suzanne used to live. I was sure she was well loved by all, and that they wanted to say goodbye to her one last time. I briefly wondered how they could have come here, as most of them were very old, but then I saw two taxis with their red lights on and their chauffeurs — who were both outside their cabs talking together — and figured they'd be waiting there until the end of the ceremony.

Right then the hearse pulled up in the gravel covered driveway leading to the church. I had a huge lump in my throat when I realized that it was my beloved grandmother who was inside that varnished box.

It was a very moving funeral service. My mother, choked up with sobs, read a eulogy she'd written.

When it was over we all accompanied Grandma Suzanne to the village cemetery, located about a quarter of a mile from the church. That was when my phone in my purse vibrated. I glanced at it and saw that it was Captain Delahousse who'd left me a voicemail. I didn't want to listen to it now and put it back.

I was astonished to see that those two taxis were in the funeral procession too. They probably were there to pick their clients back up after the ceremony, so they wouldn't have to walk back to the church.

I was even more surprised when after the casket was put into the ground, where I bawled like a little kid, one of the two chauffeurs, as did the family members and friends who were at the ceremony, walked up to express his condolences to me. Except that rather than just saying he was sorry for my loss, as I was expecting from someone I'd never seen before, he surprised me.

"I'm probably one of the last persons to have seen your grandmother alive."

"Excuse me?" I jumped, troubled.

"I'm a taxi driver. I'm the one who drove your sweet grandmother back here, the day after your wedding. You must be Colombe? She talked about you for the whole ride back."

"I am," I said with a broken voice.

"Just as charming as how she described you. I even accompanied her back to her room."

"Thank you," I said, waiting for the next person to come and shake my hand.

But the man, a bit invasive, visibly hadn't yet finished.

"She seemed to be such a nice lady. I was only with her for about half an hour, but she made a big impression on me. A lady with character, a sense of humor too, I think. What a loss. Please accept my deepest sympathy."

"Thanks."

He must have understood by the tone of my voice that he was monopolizing me, and I wanted to speak with those I actually knew and walked away. That guy, someone I'd never seen in my life, left me slightly uncomfortable. His penetrating glaze, his incongruous and strange attitude, troubled me, without being able to put my finger on the reason why.

It was only later that I understood the origin of my troubles.

When I got back home and listened to Captain Delahousse's message.

CHAPTER 20
Signs of a break-in

"MRS. Bastaro, Captain Delahousse here. I hope I'm not bothering you. I just wanted to tell you about the progress we've made in our investigation about the death of your grandmother. I sent one of my guys there and asked him to sniff around and ask some official questions. I'd like to talk to you about that. Could you call me back when you get this message? Thanks."

"Captain Delahousse? Colombe Bastaro. I got your message, I was at my grandmother's funeral when you called."

"Oh, sorry... and sorry for your loss."

"You made some progress then?"

"Yes and no."

"Meaning?"

"Like I told you, I sent one of my men over to see if he could find more about your grandmother's sudden death, one that seemed too full of coincidences to your eyes."

"And I'm still convinced that it's much too sudden to be completely natural."

"Well, I'm personally convinced of the opposite. There was nothing suspicious at all. There were no signs of a break-in or anything like that on your grandmother's door. Plus to open it, you need an electronic badge, all the residents wear them, and they're required to enter, not to leave. The employees didn't note anything abnormal the day or night before she passed. As for the doctor, he didn't find any traces of violence. Mrs. Bastaro, her death occurred in completely normal circumstances. It was that time for your grandma, if that can make you feel any better."

"Her time..." I mechanically repeated to myself.

"Ah! There was one little unimportant thing though. That one of the nurses' aides, named Marie who was working that Sunday when your grandmother got back to the residence after your wedding, told us. She said she was surprised to stumble upon a man she'd never seen before who was escorting your grandmother to her room. Which is something forbidden by the rules and regulations, except for family members. She told us it was the taxi driver who..."

"A taxi driver," I nearly shouted. "Now that's a coincidence."

"Excuse me?"

"Meaning that I literally just got back from the funeral and at the cemetery, when it was over, some unknown man walked up to express his condolences to me and kept on talking and told me that he was one of the last persons to have seen my grandma Suzanne alive. Don't you think that's strange? And after that are you going to tell me again that I'm imagining coincidences wherever I go?"

"Mrs. Bastaro," the captain tried to calm her, "I didn't say anything like that. Coincidences are a part of our daily lives and it's actually sometimes because of them that we have a satisfactory ending to some of our investigations. Sometimes for example our men will be ticketing an automobilist because of illegal parking and then they'll realize that he's someone they've been looking for a holdup or a homicide."

That cop who was constantly trying to minimize my suggestions was really getting on my nerves now.

"Still," I continued dryly, "you don't think that's kind of weird that a guy I have never seen in my entire life comes to my grandmother's funeral and then won't stop yakking?"

"What are you trying to say, Mrs. Bastaro? Are you accusing this man of something? Like having assassinated your grandmother? Of having written those threatening letters? I've got the impression that you've been seeing evil everywhere for the past three days."

"Because you think I'm exaggerating? Dammit, put yourself in my shoes!"

"Calm down. I do understand you. But what I'm trying to say is that that man was probably just trying to be nice and show compassion to the family of an old lady he appreciated. Nothing more, nothing less."

"Okay, but as for me, I'd like you to question that man. I'm sure he has lots of interesting things to say. Could you do that for me, Captain?"

I heard the policeman sighing loudly on the other end of the line, as if he was getting tired of talking about his case and what I was asking him.

"I'll try to learn more about him. But we still have to find that guy. Right now, all we have is a vague description that one of the employees of the nursing home gave us. She said he was a young man, about thirty, quite tall, blond hair, large shoulders. Do you confirm that?"

"Yes, that does correspond to the description of the man who came up to me in the cemetery."

"Could you describe his vehicle? You wouldn't happen to have his license plate?"

"You're joking, right? That's the least of my worries now. And I'm not trying to be rude, but I think that's your job, isn't it? By the way, did you get the email I transferred to you?"

"My guys are working on it. We're trying to follow its electronic current up to the sender, but that's not going to be an easy task. This guy takes a lot of precautions. I'll let you know of any progress we make. And in the meanwhile, you be careful, Mrs. Bastaro."

I hung up, still frustrated. I felt so powerless faced with that vague and intangible threat hanging over us and our ninety-nine guests we'd invited to our wedding. If Grandma Suzanne did die a natural death, that meant the threat was continuing.

Plus I knew that the police were incapable of protecting everyone. As long as we couldn't identify the author of those threats, it would be nearly impossible for us to determine who was the target he was aiming at.

Or... the targets.

CHAPTER 21
With our nerves

HE WASN'T GIVING us a single break.

The day after Grandma Suzanne's funeral, we received a new message, even more enigmatic this time.

The same sender's name, ***Anonymousemail***, impossible to track down.

The same horrifying, sickening tone, that fake sympathy when addressing us. The way he was always playing with our nerves with his disgusting civilities.

There was an attachment, a virtual e-card.

THOUGH FLOWERS WILT, die, and disappear, their beautiful perfumes are always present. Just like these beautiful flowers, those that we love never die; they always remain with us, reflected in our precious memories.

. . .

That crappy prose, something you could see on a cheap grave marker, probably copied from a manual of polite formulas, made me sick. I felt like throwing up on those words.

"That scumbag!"

But the message didn't end there. There was more after a line feed.

More that I didn't want to read, but that of course drew my eyes to it by its enigmatic aspect.

As life goes on, and we have to advance in spite of the departure of our loved ones, I'd like to invite you, my dear Colombe, my dear Jerome, to continue with our riddles. Little by little, after each of my messages, you'll make progress, I'm sure of that, and you'll solve them. When we get to that point, what I call the moment of truth will arrive.

Here's the next mystery, if you accept it. After words, let's play with numbers, see how I like varying pleasures! When you play with me, you'll never be bored!

1-1
6-4
7-1
11-3
11-5
15-4
16-2
18-2
20-2

24-2
Have fun!
And see you soon...

"This guy should be locked up!" Jerome exclaimed, furious.

"That's for sure," I agreed despondently.

We looked at our phones, with the figures and numbers dancing in an infernal sarabande.

"Now what is he trying to make us understand?" I continued, already starting to draw up a few hypotheses.

"It instinctively makes me think of tennis scores, you see, those 1-1, 6-4, etc.," Jerome who was a good player, thought out loud.

"7-1?"

"No. There's never that score. 7-5 or 7-6, those would be possible. That could happen with a tie-break, but a score of 7-1 would be impossible. But for the others, if you want to stay in the field of sports, for 11-3 or 11-5, that makes me think of table tennis. And 15-4 makes me think of badminton. As for what follows, I have no idea. Or maybe results of rugby or football, why not?"

I didn't know much about sports and how their points were tallied up, so I couldn't help Jerome here.

"Why keep on seeing scores? I can't see any link with us. All that's Greek to me."

That must have rung a bell someplace in Jerome's brain.

"Greek? Hey, don't we have a Bible someplace here?"

"We do, even a Koran. I've read both of them. On the bookshelves in our bedroom, why?"

Jerome got up and scurried in. He came back with a thick book, one with a beige cover on it and that I knew well, as when I was at the university, I'd read it all and had highlighted or written notes about countless paragraphs in the one thousand three hundred pages it contained.

Now I understood what he was getting at!

"Bible verses!"

My sweetie sat down next to me and opened up the book to the first chapter.

Genesis. The beginning of everything. Maybe where we should start looking? That suddenly seemed obvious to me.

— *1-1. In the beginning God created the heavens and the earth,* I recited to myself by memory.

Jerome silently agreed, feverishly turning the pages, before stopping to read the next one.

— *6-4. The Nephilim were on the earth in those days, and also afterward, when the sons of God came in to the daughters of men, and they bore children to them. These were the mighty men that were of old, the men of renown.*

One after another, our noses in the yellowed paper

of that sacred book, we read and recopied the verses at the same time.

— *7-1. Then the Lord said to Noah, "Go into the ark, you and all your household, for I have seen that you are righteous before me in this generation."*

— *11-3. And the said to one another, "Come, let us make bricks and burn them thoroughly." And they had brick for stone and bitumen for mortar.*

— *11-5. And the Lord came down to see the city and the tower, which the sons of men had built.*

— *15-4. And behold, the word of the Lord came to him, "This man shall not be your heir, your own son shall be your heir."*

— *16-2. And Sar'ai said to Abram, "Behold now, the Lord has prevented me from having children; go into my maid; it may be that I shall obtain children by her." And Abram harkened to the voice of Sar'ai.*

— *18-2. He lifted up his eyes to look and behold, three men stood in front of him. When he saw them he ran from the tent door to meet them and bowed himself to the earth.*

— *20-2. And Abraham said of Sara, his wife, "She is my sister." And Abim'elech, king of Gerar sent and took Sara.*

— *24-1. Now Abraham was old, well-advanced in years; and the Lord had blessed Abraham in all things.*

Reading all those Bible verses had left us

dumbfounded, even more lost than we had been five minutes ago.

What on earth could those disparate verses taken from the first book of the Bible, that time-independent Genesis, mean? What conclusions could they give us about our problem? Those ten short excerpts seemed vague and general to me. They talked about God, Abraham, Sara, Noah and the first men on Earth. We couldn't make heads nor tails of it, seemingly. We looked around for some keywords that could give us a lead we could work on, but nothing popped out to us. I wondered if that was correct.

"Why would those numbers have to refer to Genesis? I think that they're all over in the Old and in the New Testament... How can we know where to look?"

"Wait a second. You said, 'those numbers?'"

"I did. Because they seem like numbers to me."

Jerome went to the table of contents and found the number of the page he was looking for. The book of Numbers!

All excited about his new idea, we did the same thing, reading and recopying the verses in that part of the fourth book of the Pentateuch. 1-1; 6-4; 7-1; etc.

There again, ten sentences that didn't inspire us. They talked about grapevines, cucumbers, melons, leeks, tabernacles, flour, oil, a body of water, Moses, and Israel.

Except for maybe a recipe, we were unable to decipher anything that was intelligible.

"What's irking me," said Jerome, "is that we could do this in nearly all the parts of this book."

"Plus, there's nothing telling us that we should be looking in the Bible," I completed. "Well, I've got a stupid idea, let's see if it's worth anything. As Jerome is your first name, why don't we look into the Book of Prophets, into Jeremiah?

For the third time, with however a bit less enthusiasm than during the first two, we began to leaf through the Book of Jeremiah. Once again, a huge failure. Except maybe the 6-4 that could have applied. *"Prepare war against her; Up! And let us attack at noon!"*

I just sighed, ready to give up.

"*Pff*, now what? He's trying to tell us that he'll attack someone at noon?"

"Hmm. I doubt it, I don't think there's any evidence of that."

We were both beginning to lose hope and curse even more the author of that stupid game.

"So now what?" I asked impatiently.

"Now I don't know anymore," Jerome said, putting the Bible down.

"I'm exhausted. I just want this nightmare to end."

Still, I knew that it had just begun. Jerome took me in his arms, kissed me on my forehead while stroking my hair.

"It'll come to us," he promised. "You know what? We're gonna forget this damn enigma and go outside, that'll do us good."

I was on the point of giving into his suggestion when my eyes looked down one last time on the verses of Genesis that we'd copied.

One of them jumped out at me as if it had been lit up by a blinking neon light at the county fair.

The 20-2.

And Abraham said of Sara, his wife, "She is my sister." And Abim'elech, king of Gerar sent and took Sara.

"She is my sister."
 And took Sara.

"Oh no!" I said.

"My sister's name is Sara...
 Just like in the Bible."

CHAPTER 22
The scene of a nightmare

MY SISTER SARA, Damien, her husband, and my niece Justine, lived in a little town in the hills overlooking Marseille, called Rousset. A large village or little town, depending on the point of view of the person talking about it, with Mont Sainte Victoire on one side of it and the vineyards and olive trees on the other side. Your ideal and picture-perfect French Provincial landscape.

One that could become the scene of a nightmare.

"We don't have a choice now," I said soberly. "We have to tell Sara that she's in danger."

I was going to pick up my phone when Jerome grabbed my hand.

"Wait a sec. Your conclusion just stems from our very quick deductions, almost brainstorming. We might be completely wrong here. In which case we'd scare your sister for nothing."

"But darn it Jerome, we can't just stand here with our arms crossed, waiting for him to hit us again."

"Again?"

"I'm still convinced that Grandma Suzanne didn't die because of her old age."

"Stop it, Colombe, stop torturing yourself like that. The cops and the doctors were formal, she died a natural death. Period. I know it's difficult to admit that there are so many coincidences, — or here maybe I should say conjunctions — in this story, but we have to admit it."

I got up and started walking around in circles in the room, my mind tortured with questions.

"Okay. Let's admit that then. It's true, like that bastard says, that his game has just begun and I'm afraid he's right. If that's so, then the victim hasn't yet been chosen, but for me they were pointed out in the last message. *She is my sister.* That's what was written. *And took Sara.* Does that seem clear enough to you? This guy is getting ready to kidnap my sister Sara. And that can't be just another coincidence. I have to warn her."

Jerome sighed and nodded his head in a sign of acquiescence, then handed me my phone.

"This was bound to happen," he declared. "We couldn't keep a secret like that till the end without warning the potential victims. Go ahead, call her."

I grabbed my phone and put in my sister's name. We rarely called each other. We appreciated each other, but that was life, you could say we loved each other without daring to say it. I nonetheless read in her eyes a couple of days ago, during our wedding, how happy she was to see her little sister wearing her white wedding gown.

Her phone rang five times before going to voicemail.

"This is Sara's cell phone, please leave me a message." Sober, simple, just like she was.

I heard the "beep" in my ear and the silence of the phone met mine, in the exasperating expectation of my first words that I didn't seem able to pronounce.

What was I going to say?

"Go into hiding Sara, there's some crazy guy who's after you."

A bit abrupt, don't you think? Neither founded, nor believable.

I took a deep breath and finally spit out a few words, unsteadily.

"Sara, it's Colombe. Call me back when you get this message. Bye. Love you."

Those last words made me choke up. I quickly hung up so she wouldn't hear me sobbing on the phone.

While I had my phone out, I transferred the email I'd received a few minutes ago to Captain Delahousse.

After that, we spent an hour or so writing that list of our guests that he'd asked us for.

Each time we wrote a new name down, it sparked a new twinge of sorrow in our hearts. I was wondering if I wasn't writing the name of the next person who would be his victim. The policeman had asked us to indicate all the contact details for everyone, their address, phone number, email or anything else we thought could be useful to them to reach them.

My eyes teared up again when I was getting ready to write down Suzanne's name, and I crossed it out. When we'd finished, I put everything into a Word document.

During all that time I kept wondering when Sara would call me back. I needed to know that she was alright. But after an hour with no news from her, I decided to call her back.

Once again, no answer except for her voicemail message.

"She must still be at work," my husband said.

I looked at my watch.

"I'd say that she must be back by now. Why isn't she answering?"

"How the heck should I know?" Jerome answered, now irritated. "She's got a life! She could be at a doctor's appointment, shopping, at the gym or at a Tupperware party with her friends, who knows!"

"Okay, let's not argue. But can you understand that I'm freaking out? Shit!"

"Of course I understand! I have feelings too, you know! I'm just trying to put things into their context. Not overreacting, with the tiniest word, gesture, the most minute situation that's a bit unusual. It's not the first time that your sister doesn't answer right away when you call her or doesn't call back immediately."

"Forget it. I'll take care of this myself."

"Stop that! That's not what I said."

This was one of the very first times we had raised our voices. This situation was getting so stressful that both of us were cranky. I sighed and held my hand out towards Jerome's.

"I'm so sorry," I told him tenderly.

"So am I," he confirmed just like Patrick Swayze in *Ghost*, a movie that made us cry each time we watched it, said.

"I'm going to call Damien."

I looked up my brother-in-law's number in my contacts list. He picked up after his phone had rung three times.

"Hey hey! Colombe, how are things? Are you on your honeymoon? Calling me from the white sand beach in Cancun?" he joked.

If only he'd known that I had other fish to fry rather than working on my tan on a Mexican beach on the Caribbean seaside! I got straight to the point.

"Hi Damien. Sorry to bother you, but do you know where my sister is? I've been trying to reach her for an hour, but she hasn't picked up or called me back. At this time of day she must be back from work."

"She had a day off today," Damien replied. "She went to Marseille this afternoon, to do some shopping with one of her friends. How come? You had something important to ask her? Maybe I can help."

"That's nice of you Damien, but I'd like to speak with her directly. Do you know when she'll be back?

Who knows, maybe her batterie is dead. Can I call you on your landline later?"

There was a silence at the other end of the line, my sister's husband must have been looking at what time it was on his phone or on the clock in their kitchen.

"That is strange. She should have been back an hour ago round about, at least that was what was planned. Maybe there are traffic jams exiting Marseille or on the tollway. I'm sure she'll be back soon. I'll give her your message as soon as she walks in. So, everything's fine with you two lovebirds?"

"It is," I lied. "Fine."

"Do you want to speak to your niece? She just got back from gym."

I couldn't bring myself to speak to my sweet little niece, Justine.

"I have to hang up now, I'll call back later. Thanks, Damien."

"No problem. Say hi to Jerome for us."

I hung up, lowered my head and put my hands on it. I summed up the conversation for Jerome.

"He doesn't know where Sara is, and she should have been back an hour ago. This doesn't sound good…"

CHAPTER 23
The throbbing heart

THAT THIRTY-SOME-YEAR-OLD LOVED SPENDING an afternoon in town with her friend. Window shopping was so much more fun when both of you liked it. Trying on clothes, without actually buying them, just for the pleasure of looking at yourself in the mirrors in shops, wearing much too expensive though very sexy dresses. The type of clothing you don't wear every day, but for very precise events, dresses that cling to your skin, tight skirts that flaunt your figure. Because everyone always wants to please, even if you're just pleasing yourself.

That was exactly what Sara was doing that afternoon, shopping near the Marseille port. Sitting outside on a patio of one of the many cafés on the Quay de la Joliette, she was sipping on a raspberry mojito with her colleague Malika, someone who'd become her friend after years of working together. Across from them, the sun slowly began to shine on the Basilia of Notre Dame de la Garde, affectionately called "The Good Mother" by those living in Marseille.

"This outing with just the two of us did me a world of good," said Sara. "We should do this more often, don't you think?"

"It should even be reimbursed by our health insurance," Malika added.

Sara leaned back on her chair, the sun on her face, and closed her eyes. She felt so good right then, with her friend, far from her everyday little worries and abstractions. She let her mind drift. With her eyes closed, she heard the sounds of the city — scooters backfiring, horns beeping, tiny waves lapping against boats — as well as laughter next to her and a few wolf whistles aimed at her long legs.

She knew men liked her, with or without a sexy dress. At the age of thirty-five, she was at her peak, in the years where many people said that women became more beautiful at each birthday. Sara knew that nearly every day men, barely pubescent ones or already sporting gray hair, would turn around to look at her, follow her with their eyes, even rubbernecking so they wouldn't miss a thing. She was both proud but had a bit of contempt when she saw they were afraid to frankly come up to her. In a nutshell, she possessed an inaccessible beauty, one that attracted men while intimidating them.

Every once in a while, someone would try something. Also every once in a while, if she felt like it, she'd agree to have a glass of wine with them on a patio. But it never went farther than that.

Till now.

She glanced at her phone.

"Darn, I don't have any battery left. Malika, what time is it?"

"Six thirty."

"Oh shoot, I'm going to be late," Sara said.

She rounded her lips around the straw in her mojito and quickly finished the last inch or so. Then she picked up her bags, put her purse over her shoulder and said goodbye to Malika.

"We'll do it again as soon as possible," Malika promised.

Sara smiled at her friend and sent her an air kiss as she walked away from the bar. She walked to the parking lot where she'd parked her red Kadjar three hours ago, an elegant SUV that was popular with young women like her.

She passed the La Major Cathedral towards the Vieux Port, then turned in front of the Mucem's parking lot where she'd left her car, on the third sublevel. Though it was a bit pricey, it was an ideal location when you wanted to walk around in the city's throbbing heart.

She hated underground parking lots, as a kid she'd

been claustrophobic. A bunch of teens were hanging around near the automatic pay stations. They all stared at her when she stopped in front of the machine. She even thought she heard a couple of words about how short her skirt was, how luscious her red lips were and how beautiful her long brown hair was. She tried to ignore them, taking her credit card out of her wallet, then curiously putting it back in again without paying.

She waited for the elevator and quickly went in, relieved to have left that little gang of impolite teens upstairs.

She went downstairs to the third sublevel, one that was quite dark despite the lights here and there. She looked for the row where she'd parked her Kadjar, place 322, she remembered. That floor seemed to be deserted, though it wasn't late. She heard her heels click-clacking on the sad concrete floor, resonating eerily. She kept turning her head right to left each time she thought she heard someone else's steps. She sure didn't appreciate underground parking lots.

She finally spotted her car, and her pace quickened, so she could quickly shelter herself inside. She rummaged around in her purse, looking for her electronic key and pressed the remote unlock button. A few steps in front of her, her car beeped, and its back lights blinked three times.

She opened the door, got in, tossed her purse onto the passenger seat, and centrally locked the doors. She put her hands on the steering wheel, took a deep breath and closed her eyes.

Then she frowned in frustration when she couldn't find the cord to charge her phone in the car.

She was running late and couldn't tell her husband.

Tough luck. What did people do before cell phones were invented, when there were only phone booths that you couldn't even find anywhere today?

She dithered for a few minutes, as if paralyzed by indecision. She was shaking, without really knowing why. She was afraid of something, but what? People are always afraid of anything unknown, new, definitive.

She inspected, through the car window, the empty cars around her as well as the lot where some shadows were coming and going.

Then she tried to relax, giving herself a few minutes to calm down and let her heartbeat decelerate.

She suddenly screamed when someone tapped on her window.

She thought her heart was about to stop.

There was a man standing there and his massive body blocked the light.

He put a hand on the door handle and pulled it. When he saw that it was locked, his gaze hardened and he pulled it again, several times, as if by doing this the door would suddenly open.

"Get out!" he articulated slowly.

CHAPTER 24
Emergency!

WHEN THE PHONE RANG, two hours later, we were both alarmed, our fears had been founded. My brother-in-law's name was on the screen and as soon as I picked up I could tell how worried he was.

"It's nine o'clock and Sara's still not here and I can't get through to her!"

"What?" I asked stupidly. Deep down inside though I'd known this would happen, I had a gut feeling.

"Sara hasn't come back home yet," Damien said, carefully articulating each word. "She should have been back two hours ago. I listened to the traffic news, there weren't more traffic jams than usual on the tollway. I can't understand that she didn't try to call me if she had some sort of problem. A breakdown, a fender bender, something like that."

"Did she tell you where she was going?"

"Yeah, like I told you earlier, she was going to

Marseille to do some shopping with one of her friends."

"And did you call that friend?" I asked, immediately cutting him off.

"Yeah, and Malika told me they'd spent the afternoon together. They went into the shops, had a glass to drink on the patio of a café, nothing special, girl stuff. She told me they both left about six-thirty. And she added that Sara suddenly realized it was later than she thought, and she left really quickly. And she hasn't heard from her since then."

"She didn't add anything else in particular that rang a bell someplace?"

"I don't think so. Ah! Yes, she said that Sara's cell phone was dead."

"Which explains why she didn't answer us when we called," I thought out loud. "And she wouldn't have been able to tell you about any problems she had on the road."

I heard Damien huffing and puffing tensely.

"No, I don't agree. There's always a possibility to have someone lend you a phone, or to go into a store or a bar and use theirs."

Then I remembered the verses of the Bible we'd noted down.

And took Sara.

"But she would have had to be able to move freely and be conscious then," I laconically said.

"What do you mean?"

I was now at the tipping point. If I wanted to

develop my idea to my sister's husband, I'd have to spill the beans. Was this the right time? Didn't he have enough to be concerned about without me adding something? Nonetheless, not telling him anything wouldn't do any good either. Jerome, sitting across from me, nodded to encourage me, and I decided to invite Damien into the very closed circle of those who knew we had been threatened.

"Damien, something really unusual happened after our wedding. Something that could be linked with Sara's disappearance."

"What the hell are you talking about?"

"I know, and that could seem absurd or completely unreal to you, but that's been our sad reality since Sunday. Please Damien, just listen carefully to me without interrupting me, and you'll be able to see for yourself."

I told my brother-in-law everything that had happened in those past four days. How we discovered the first letter in the urn in the banquet hall, the anonymous letters we'd received in our mailbox and the anonymous emails as well, all the troubling coincidences in the death of Grandma Suzanne, and how the cops were unable to find any leads on that "terrorist." Then I continued to the last message we'd received and had interpreted — though we weren't sure of anything of course — to be Bible verses which had led us to think that perhaps Sara was in danger. Sara, his wife, who no one had seen since the end of the afternoon.

"That's ridiculous!" Damien said. "You guys are

completely nuts! Something like that can't be true. Sara can't be involved in something like that. She must have had some problem that's easily explainable. Maybe she was injured, or she fainted, and they took her to a hospital. I'm gonna start calling them now..."

Damien was speaking faster and faster, the speed of his words betrayed how nervous he actually was, that he was in denial, that he couldn't face reality. Of course I did understand that he refused to believe our theory. Even us, though we had been immersed up to our necks in this for the past few days, we were having problems realizing that it was true. We were facing situations that ordinarily only took place in novels or in movies, not *in real life*, not in ordinary people's daily lives!

Yet it was happening.

"You should try to call the hospitals in Marseille," I told Damien. "And then the police too, to declare Sara's disappearance. That's what I'm going to do on my side with Captain Delahousse, who's been on this case since the beginning. He could liaison with services that are..."

"Hey!" he cut me off. "Come back to earth, Colombe! No cop will open a file about the disappearance of a thirty-five-year-old adult who's three hours late. You know as well as I do that thousands of adults disappear each year in France. People who are sick and tired of their shitty lives, and decide to up and go, to start over. Or who leave for a day or two, a week, then come back. If the cops opened a file for each of them, that's all they'd do. And believe me, they've got plenty of other stuff, especially in Marseille."

"But I'm telling you it was written in the Bible!" I shouted.

I could hear him laughing nervously.

"And why not refer to Nostradamus and his predictions while you're at it?"

"Damien, this isn't a laughing matter. I'm serious. We have to do something, you and me both. This is an emergency!"

CHAPTER 25
Her last moments

DAMIEN FINALLY DECIDED to report his wife as missing. And we also contacted Captain Delahousse, who this time took our assumptions seriously. After he'd received the copy of the latest email, he said he would now take our reflections based on those Bible verses into consideration, as for the moment he had no other leads.

He seemed open to our theory and understanding about how worried we were about Sara. Even though, and I'm quoting him here, it could well have been another unfortunate coincidence. But the opposite could have been true too, meaning my sister had been kidnapped.

The captain contacted his counterparts in Marseille and then got in touch with my brother-in-law, as well as Malika, Sara's girlfriend, who seemed to have been the last person to have seen her... free and alive.

After that, the investigators started searching for anything they could find about the last known moments of Sara when she was in Marseille. Thanks to what Malika told them, they sent men off to question employees of the shops where the two ladies had gone to, as well as that café where they'd had a drink together.

They were able to retrace a timetable of where Sara had been and when. Malika had told them that she always parked her car in the Mucem Museum underground parking lot, and they then contacted the company that managed it. Using the surveillance system that filmed and logged the plates of cars coming in and leaving, they were able to determine that Sara's Kadjar had entered the lot at 3:36 pm and... had never left.

A duo of policemen was sent to the site to see if the car was still there.

Which they confirmed, no doubt about that. In the third sublevel of the lot, place 322, a red Kadjar with the license plate they were looking for was still there that evening, at 11:42 pm.

Inside...

CHAPTER 26
Declared dead

... NO ONE!

The policemen from Marseille's second district, who had been sent to the Mucem's parking lot, discovered that the car's doors weren't locked.

Using a flashlight, they inspected the car through its windows, looking at the seats, rugs, the dashboard, for any clues they could exploit. There seemingly was nothing suspicious, except for the fact that the car was unlocked in a public underground parking lot smack in the middle of Marseille. Open and accessible to anyone and everyone.

One of the two agents put a pair of latex gloves on and put his hand on the car door handle on the driver's side. He opened the door and by professional reflex, began to feel in between the backrests of the seats and the seat itself, hoping to find something that could help him understand what could have happened in that car. Outside of an old shopping receipt dated two months ago and a barrette, there wasn't anything. He looked over the entire inside of the vehicle, from bottom to top, fearing that he'd find some traces of a fight, blood or other corporal liquids, but the car was clean. A vehicle that was well kept up and that smelled good, like a woman's perfume.

Nothing to make him fear anything. And nothing to indicate that the owner of the Kadjar had had any problems.

But still, she had vanished hours ago. Without contacting her husband or anyone else.

Sara had simply disappeared, vanished.

Into thin air.

In the car at least, neither of the policemen found a single thing that could have explained her absence.

Nonetheless, though there were no signs she was alive, at least right now there were no signs that she was dead either.

Following the example of that legal formula everyone knows, *Every person charged with an offence shall be deemed to be innocent until such time as they have been found guilty*, in Sara's case, the investigators as well as those close to her, had to presume she was alive until such time as she had been declared dead. That undoubtedly was a mere truism, but it was what was the most realistic for now.

As the day drew to an end, there were no clues, no messages, nothing that could affirm that the young lady had been kidnapped, opposed to what her husband feared. Thus when the two cops went back to the station to write up their report, they could only conclude that the young lady was missing, though she seemed to have abandoned her car in the parking lot without even locking it.

With no other developments, the case for the moment was closed to her husband Damien's dismay.

∾

Despite the fact it was late at night — his phone displayed a bit after one in the morning —, he had just hung up with the police station in Marseille's second district. The news was not good. The policeman however had tried to quell his fears.

"Mr. Lesueur, let me reassure you on one point. Though we have no idea where your wife is, there's nothing that indicates she's in danger. You know, there are loads of adults who disappear each year in France. In cop speak this is what we refer to as voluntary disappearances of capable persons."

"Capable of what?"

"By that we mean people who are adults and not protected, not under some form of guardianship, for example. If so, their disappearance is immediately deemed to be a disappearance giving rise to concern. That's not the case for your wife, is it?"

"Of course not! But that doesn't mean her disappearance doesn't worry me! You know why I contacted you. I know this can seem crazy, but now I'm persuaded that what happened to my cousin since she got married is linked to my wife's disappearance. Dammit, you have to do something!"

"Please calm down, Mr. Lesueur. I understand how angry you are. In the vast majority of cases, people who go missing turn up, at their homes or elsewhere, in just a couple of days. Often they have just run away, they needed a break, or something like that. Tell me, Mr. Lesueur, has your wife seemed to be depressed recently? Has she had any mood swings, or unusual words or actions, any signs whatsoever that could explain the fact that she didn't come back home last night and didn't tell anyone where she was? Did you two get into a fight?"

Damien had to bite his lip so he wouldn't shout at the policeman's terrible words. What the hell was he imagining? That Sara took off because she hated her life and family? And what about Justine, their adorable little girl? Does a mother abandon the fruit of her womb on the spur of the moment? That to make a long story short was what he was trying to tell the cop.

"I know all of that, Mr. Lesueur. Here's what we can do. I'll mail you a *Cerfa* form to fill in, and that will allow us to open an administrative investigation to start out with. This is called a *request to note the presumption of absence*."

"I love French administration," complained the abandoned husband.

"Sorry for the jargon, but that's the name of the document. Fill it out to your best, with any elements you'd like to communicate to us and send it back to me as soon as possible. Then we'll be able to log Sara into our file of missing persons. For the moment, that's all we can legally do."

"Paperwork? That's all you can do? Jesus Christ, someone kidnapped my wife, that's what that anonymous message her sister Colombe Bastaro received said! *And took Sara*, that's what was written in the Bible."

"Mr. Lesueur, I hate to remind you, but France is a secular State, and the Bible isn't recognized in our laws. Plus, if I understood correctly, this is just something that your sister-in-law thought *could* possibly be true. For me this is just a coincidence. I'd bet anything that your wife turns up tomorrow, safe and sound, and that she can explain everything."

Damien sighed loudly, trying to convince himself mentally.

"I sure hope you're right," he said after giving his email to the policeman.

CHAPTER 27
Unlimited shame

A THIN SHEET barely hiding her nude body, Sara was floating in the vapors of unconsciousness.

She felt lost, disoriented.

In such a short lapse of time, how could she have found herself in a situation like that?

Her entire body was aching, just as if she'd been beaten. Lying on a bed, she turned her head to the side and looked at the digital alarm clock: 3:21 a.m. She understood a bit better why she was so exhausted, both physically and mentally. Quite understandable after an endless day like that.

The young lady wanted to turn around, raise one of her legs over the other to pivot and get into a more comfortable position, on her stomach, but couldn't. She could not cross her legs, and a sharp pain irradiated through her ankles. Her head was spinning, she didn't understand what was happening.

It was as if she was drunk.

Or drugged?

She couldn't remember a thing. She couldn't remember precisely what had happened in the past hours. Human brains sometimes have strange ways of working, she thought to herself, trying to sit up to see why her ankles couldn't move. But rather than being able to raise her bust, all she could do was to raise her head, and even then, just barely, because now her wrists were killing her.

Out of the corner of her eye she saw that her ankles were tied up by scarves, long ones tied down to the sculpted feet of the wooden bed. The same thing for her arms, tied to the bed by a pair of handcuffs whose steel was biting painfully into her skin. That was where that confused feeling of burning that had fleetingly woken her up from the torpidity in which she had been bathing till now came from.

Understanding her situation, prevented from moving at all, nude below the minute thickness of the sheet and already crippled by cramps in all four members, she tried to shout while struggling to get out.

Not a single sound came out though.

Her shout perhaps came through her lips, but didn't go through the thickness of the cloth covering her mouth.

Gagged, fettered, nude and dizzy, Sara began to panic.

Her eyes opened disproportionately as her brain began to assimilate the situation she was in. Her head turned to one side, then the other, scrutinizing the room, dimly lit by a small bedside lamp with a shade on it. She saw a white ceiling, yellowish beige walls. Pee yellow, she stupidly thought. No decoration on the walls, not a picture frame, not a lamp, not a mirror. The austerity of a nun's bedroom, all that was missing was a crucifix above the bed. She stretched her neck backwards to make sure there actually wasn't one. Remnants of her Christian upbringing made her horribly embarrassed to be in this position and unclothed like that, so had Christ himself dominated her with His Sainthood, she would have had a totally unlimited shame. To her relief, the crucifix was absent.

And her shame with it. Though...

She couldn't move nor escape this room, one she didn't recognize, even call out for help, all she could do was try to listen. At least, she noted with relief, they hadn't put earplugs in to totally isolate her from the outside world.

A world she tried to analyze with the very few elements she had. A bed, handcuffs, a gag, her nude body, her clothes that she didn't see next to her. A bedside table with an alarm clock on it and a glass half-filled with what seemed to her to be water. On the bed itself, besides that sheet sloppily thrown over her body, there was an unusual object that suddenly attracted her attention and sparked furious questions.

Corroborating that feeling of unease she'd had ever since she'd woken up in that empty room.

Lying against her left thigh, an oblong object,

about eight inches long and a good two inches wide, impressed her. Slightly curved and ribbed on its entire length with something that looked like veins, its latex matter seemed almost lifelike to her, because of its flesh colors. Sara had seen stuff like that in movies, in some catalogues or on the web, but none like that one in real life. Luckily for her Christ wasn't above her bed, she thought, relieved, once again.

The young nude lady instinctively and with a prudish reflex, squeezed her thighs together as hard as she could. That was when she felt a sticky substance between her legs, sort of like some tacky liquid that was drying, and she completely panicked. Once again she didn't understand a thing and tried to calm down so she would be able to think.

Remember.

What happened before she arrived here?

The last images she remembered were those of an afternoon spent with her friend, shopping in Marseille. Yes, that was it, now she remembered. She'd spent a couple of hours with her friend Malika, lots of window shopping and then they had a drink outside in a café on the Vieux-Port.

She was remembering now. She had a day off, Damien exceptionally took care of Justine for that afternoon, she needed a break, she had to get away for an afternoon.

Then her phone died on her and she remembered

rushing away when she realized that she was running behind.

Her footsteps resonating on the gray concrete of the third sublevel of the Mucem parking lot, searching for where she'd parked her car.

Then the face of the man she saw through the window of her Kadjar.

But that was when everything clouded over in her memory, as if that apparition had triggered her brain fog.

How could a woman like her, one that was healthy in her body and her mind, a mother, a fulfilled working girl, lose her mind?

See her life shatter into bits?

She suddenly closed her eyes and tears began to well up in the corners of her eyelids before slowly rolling down her shame filled pink cheeks. She saw Justine, four years old, in the retinas. Pain swelled up in her chest and Sara screamed out silently into her gag.

Right then the door on the other side of the room opened slowly, squeaking a bit on its rusty hinges.

There was a silhouette in the light on the other side.

Then a face in the pallid light in the room. A face she immediately recognized.

That of the man who she'd seen through her car window, in the third sublevel of the Mucem Museum parking lot.

CHAPTER 28
An explosion of pain

Summer 2008

IT WAS BECOMING AN OBSESSION.
Something he couldn't stop. Must have been hormones.

Plus the example of others, people he knew more or less, in high school. Kids kissing each other, making out behind the bushes, flirting at each break between courses.

Already in middle school, he was aroused by the vision of those couples of pimple-faced kids wearing braces, because back in the day nearly everyone needed or wanted them. When he happened upon two of them, mouth to mouth, each time that made him think of the movie Ready for Love, *one he'd watched dozens of times in his bedroom, his hand in his shorts, stirred by Sophie Marceau. He remembered that scene where teens were eating each other's lips on the dance floor and where that kid wearing braces ended up hooked to his girlfriend's mouth. Whoopsie! Yet, how he would have loved to be that guy. No, no one looked at him, no one kissed him, no one was attracted by him though he was attracted by so many girls.*

Including one in particular.

Now that they were in high school, now that he had got pubic hair, he felt ready to do it. But for him it wasn't easy.

All that was left then was his own hand to pleasure himself, because he was incapable of bringing a girl back home.

Each evening, when it was time to go to bed, he'd listen to Sardou's song, The High School Monitor:

"Back in the day,
 I was reading "The Lost Estate"
 And, after lights out,
 I was giving myself pleasure
 I was putting myself to sleep.
 I was imagining a world
 Filled with redheaded women
 I said women, not young girls..."

Nearly every night, *echoing Sardou's lyrics, he pleasured himself in his own world, and it invariably was the same young girl who he thought of in his mind while frenetically moving his hand up and down, just like an airplane pilot with Parkinson's disease...*

There, in his fantasy, she was always consenting, he

never had to insist so she'd offer herself to him, to open those moist and pulpy lips, to roll her tongue over his, to nearly smother him by eating up his mouth just like someone starving for desire.

In his head, at that moment, he was repeating the lyrics of Sardou's song, and his hand was moving faster and faster below his blanket.

Then his dreams intensified. The young girl who catalyzed his male desires went with him into the forest — he loved natural decors that excited him more than anything — and without hesitating let him guide her to a clearing with soft grass. There, she didn't refuse when he told her to kneel down in front of him while he was unbuttoning his jeans, opening them up and with a trembling hand, taking out his enormous penis. Because in his dreams, he had hefty attributes. Why dream of spaghetti when you could imagine being equipped with a brat? "Seven inches of pleasure," as the BK advertisement claimed. "It'll blow your mind away," they added.

In the reality of his bedroom, his hand became the avatar of the young girl's mouth, and he slowed down, became more gentle, less violent with his instrument of pleasure. He would even spit in his hand to make his dream more realistic, more sensory. Up to the point where he conceived a mental amalgam. He no longer knew whether he was in his bedroom or in the forest. His eyes closed, in both places, he let himself be wrapped up in a powerful solitary pleasure. His hand, her mouth, they were the same thing for his selfish desires.

Then his dream would burst like a bubble on a bar

of soap when he'd feel the first signs of relief, those uncontrollable spasms in his lower stomach, that sudden tension in his scrotum, those seconds that were impossible to control and that invariably finished by an explosion of pain, rage, pleasure and repressed desire, quickly forgotten in a paper tissue thrown into the toilet.

The bubble would burst, the clearing would transition into darkness, the young girl would vanish and his hatred for her and the entire world would surface again.

Post coïtum animal tristis est*...
Post coïtum iuvenis odiosus est†...

---

* Latin. After coitus, the animal is sad.
† Latin. After coitus, the adolescent is hateful.

CHAPTER 29
Innocence of a child

WHILE SARA WAS STRUGGLING with her internal demons a few miles from there, at the Lesueur's house, Damien was tossing and turning.

How could he have slept?

His wife had vanished into thin air.

His sister-in-law had told him a bunch of baloney, something totally improbable, quoting Bible verses that had led her to some horrible deductions.

His four-year-old daughter, sound asleep in her bedroom with its pastel walls, still had no idea about that tragedy taking place next to her, the one threatening her innocence as a child. Lucky her. The more he could put off telling her that her mom wasn't there would be the best for her. At least not now.

For now, he preferred to let her ignore that fact. At her age, it still was possible to occult a part of the truth — that sad truth — without her being aware of it. So at dinner time that night, something Damien had thrown together, when Justine asked why her mom wasn't there, he had invented a plausible reason.

"Mommy had to go to Paris for work for a couple of days. She left quickly because her boss asked her to, you understand? But before she left, Mommy told me to tell you that she loves you and she would bring you a little souvenir back."

"An Eiffel Tower?" the little girl asked, with a big yawn.

"Probably. Or who knows, maybe some outfits for your little dolls?"

Damien had felt his voice breaking up while inventing these lies. He felt guilty for having distorted the truth. Isn't it always a good idea to explain things clearly to kids? Ready to break down, admit he had no idea where Sara, her mom was, Damien finally changed his mind.

"Finish your dessert, sweetie pie. You've got school tomorrow. Mommy's thinking of you. She'll be back soon."

Just a few minutes later, after she'd brushed her teeth, he'd carried Justine, exhausted, back to her little bed, and had read her a fairy tale — but not one where a mommy died, leaving orphans or where she abandoned her offspring in the forest — before tucking her in and kissing her goodnight. He was sure she was already sleeping when he walked out.

. . .

Sara would soon be back, Damien was trying to convince himself of that, though it didn't really work.

What that policeman had said to him a few hours earlier on the phone kept on coming back in his mind, like a leitmotiv. He could have recited his questions by heart.

Tell me, Mr. Lesueur, had your wife seemed to be depressed recently? Had she had any mood swings, or unusual words or actions, any signs whatsoever that could explain the fact that she didn't come back home last night and didn't tell anyone where she was? Did you two get into a fight, have an argument?"

No, they hadn't fought recently. No, not recently.

But when he thought about it, Damien couldn't deny that the atmosphere at home had been a bit tense for the past few months and that their relationship as a couple had distended little by little, worn out like an old rope that's unraveling, thread by thread.

Yet they had everything to be happy. Jobs, a house, friends, money and a little girl who looked like both of them. Still that didn't seem to suffice. They'd known each other for ten years and undoubtedly hadn't known how to reinvent their relationship, how to rekindle those initial sparks. They'd gone out, got engaged, then got married. Since then their couple had been purring peacefully.

Perhaps too peacefully?

Nonetheless, Sara didn't seem to have any signs of depression, to answer the policeman's question. Or perhaps he simply hadn't noticed them, Damien thought bitterly. Depression, one of the scourges of the century. Something a husband might not notice in his wife? Were you always able to understand the people with whom spent your daily life? That was what Damien was asking himself retrospectively, as the hours went by.

For the past few months, Sara had been a bit more distant with him, seeking much less physical contact. As if they were bogged down by their daily routines. Work, shopping, commuting, school, nursery school, sports and activities, weekends with friends or family, here and there, the highways and the byways, like the old saying goes. All of that could spell out a slow death for a couple if you weren't careful. At night, his wife was completely exhausted though it wasn't even ten o'clock, but she always told him that ten was her psychological limit to be able to drop off to sleep. If she didn't go to bed then, she'd be tossing and turning in her bed for at least two hours, thus nibbling away the quota of sleep she required. He though was quite the night owl, and told everyone his second evening begun at ten. As the only one awake in the house, he either read or watched TV from the couch, either an old movie in streaming or a basketball match in replay. That was how he relaxed and sometimes even fell asleep before joining his wife in bed at one or two in the morning. At the other side of their king-sized bed, Sara's slow and regular breathing, while she was all curled up, moved him so much that he sometimes wanted to wake her, spoon her to enjoy the warmth of her body. Though he knew the even unconsciously, in her sleep, she would have pushed him away. For Sara, sleep was sacred: both a pleasure and a necessity.

In cases like that, the frustrated husband would mentally hum another of Sardou's songs, *After Five Years*.

After five years passed
In complete silence,
We're here, face to face,
Listening to each other think.
Listening to each other think.
The bed seems immense.
A bit of adolescence
Could bring us together.
At the end of the day, nothing's changed
Nothing's to be done over.
Because of habits,
Our bodies are exhausted.
We make love, you could say,
Every man for himself, alone.
We make love to our dead years,
And join each other silently,
Then we leave each other,
And the show is over,
Then we leave each other,
And the show is over.

. . .

Except for her, the show had never begun. So Damien hid his desire and fell asleep, turning his back to her.

The young man looked at his alarm clock and saw it was nearly four in the morning —the middle of the night — and he still hadn't had a wink of sleep.

Had Sara and he slowly turned their backs to each other? To the point that today, she'd turned her heels and disappeared from their life?

No, he didn't want to believe that theory and now preferred to believe that twisted, bizarre one that Colombe, his sister-in-law, had presented. If Sara had gone missing, she wasn't the one who instigated her disappearance. She'd been kidnapped!

The cops would be forced to admit that, just like he now did, and set off to look for her.

Damien had printed out that *Cerfa* form the policeman had emailed him. He picked up a pen and decided to fill the form in to launch the research procedure.

While doing it, he was railing against the heavy French administrative system where everything was reduced to forms, including when a loved one went missing, where people became abstract elements, numbers, boxes to be checked.

Please read attentively note N° 52123 before filling

in this form.

Your quality, you are: the spouse, a parent, a person who has strong and stable links with the person who is absent, an associate...

Please note the date on which the person who is presumed to be innocent went missing from their domicile or residence

Indicate research undertaken to find this person

Some answers were easy to give, others quite the opposite, just like the last question on that official document.

Please detail the motives that justify your request

A dozen pre-traced lines followed. Damien hesitated for a moment. How could he ever resume in twelve lines what could have led Sara to be kidnapped? How could he summarize that incredible scenario that Colombe, his sister-in-law, had concocted?

He did his best though, declared on his honor that the information given on the form was exact, dated and signed it before sending it off the email address of the policeman at the second district station.

His entire body was trembling, eaten way by nervous fatigue. He dragged himself up to his daughter's room and carefully opened the door. Justine was sleeping soundly. She looked like a little doll, unaware of the drama taking place around her.

"We'll find your mommy," whispered Damien on his daughter's doorstep. "Promise."

CHAPTER 30
Save her

IT WAS FRIDAY, only six days after our wedding, and we were more exhausted than we'd ever been in our entire lives. Who could have thought that our entire world would collapse so quickly, in just a few hours?

I'd had another nearly sleepless night, populated by nightmares, whereas Jerome had finally been able to slip into the arms of Morphea in the middle of the night.

I was looking at him sleeping, snoring softly like he did each time he was really tired, when my phone next to my pillow vibrated. I was afraid to turn it off, constantly thinking of Sara, Damien and little Justine. I saw my brother-in-law's name on the screen. I picked up while leaving the bedroom so I wouldn't wake Jerome up. I was suddenly full of hope.

"Damien, finally! Sara's back?"

A silence followed by my brother-in-law's sobs confirmed the futility of my question. I insisted.

"Tell me you've at least got some news! Tell me she called you to explain! Tell me the cops found her! Tell me that's ridiculous, Damien, but tell me something, dammit!"

"Colombe… she's not back. I don't have any news. Sara hasn't contacted anyone, hasn't contacted me."

"I was right then. My deductions were founded. She was kidnapped and now she can't alert us. I'm going to call Captain Delahousse, those cops have to do something now! We have to find her, and sooner rather than later. Maybe we've got enough time to save her."

I choked up on those last words. Save her! The image of my own sister, maybe dead while I was speaking, broke my heart and soul in two.

Damien did his best to explain the form he'd filled out last night so that an administrative investigation could be opened.

"Like that's gonna help us, the administration!" I barked angrily. "What we need is a police investigation. Get our hands on that bastard who's been harassing us since the beginning of the week and who, and I'm sure of that, was the one who kidnapped Sara."

I could feel Jerome's reassuring and warm presence behind my back, my ranting and raving unfortunately had woken him up. He hugged me, kissed my messy hair. I turned to him, and we looked each other straight in our reddish eyes. He saw Damien's name on the phone in my hand and understood. Without me having to explain anything at all to him, he knew what I was thinking and nodded, blinking, to give me his consent.

"Damien, we're coming as quickly as possible. We can't leave you like that, our arms crossed, just waiting until something happens. We'll go looking for Sara together! And we'll find her safe and sound!"

I wanted so very much to believe what I'd just said. Yes, find his missing wife; yes, deliver my sister from the claws of that insane person, the one who for some reason totally unknown to us, had decided to target our families, ruin our lives.

From the decision to its implementation, there was just one step that we immediately took. Despite the urgency of the situation, it wouldn't have been reasonable, and we did understand that, to hop in our car and drive to Rousset, where my sister lives. Having slept only a few awkward hours since Sunday, we were so exhausted that it would have been dangerous or even suicidal to drive those four hundred and fifty miles, even taking turns driving. We looked for a Bordeaux-Marseille flight and booked two seats on one that was leaving from Merignac Airport right before noon. Then, following our logic coherently, we booked a cab that would take us to the airport and asked Damien to pick us up when we arrived in Marignane. A one-hour flight maximum separated us from the place where Sara had gone missing.

We had to do something.

Just thinking about doing nothing made my legs tingle. I was sick and tired of being the prey of a sadistic puppeteer who was pulling on the strings of our destinies. I was time to cut the cord, to liberate ourselves from his diktats and to follow our instincts.

I stuffed everything I thought we'd need for a couple of days into two suitcases. I hoped to finish quickly and find Sara, though the leads we had were few and far between. We didn't know a thing about that nutjob who was manipulating us, but we now did know that he had decided to target one of the ninety-nine potential victims who'd attended our wedding, like he'd written in his introductory letter. All the following messages had merely confirmed that Sara was his unfortunate target.

Why my sister? That was the question we had to find an answer to, with Damien's help, to understand the motivations of that wacko.

WE WERE READY TO GO, our suitcases closed, house all locked up, when the taxi pulled up. We were walking towards the gate when I saw the cab. I frowned, quite intrigued. Of course, I knew that nothing looked more like a taxi than another taxi. Most taxis here in France are classy-looking sedans, the vast majority of them black, usually shiny and clean, but the one coming towards us while Jerome was closing the gate, titillated my peace of mind.

The car looked just like the one that had followed

the funeral procession for my grandma. Because of the tinted windows though, I couldn't see the driver's face.

Until he stopped the car and slowly got out.

The very second I saw his face, my heart made an unexpected stop, confirming my intuition.

I was suddenly afraid of getting in.

THE DRIVER of that taxi was the man who had spoken to me for such a long time at my Grandma Suzanne's funeral.

CHAPTER 31
False destination

I GLANCED at my watch and saw I didn't have a choice, I'd have to take this cab. If we wanted to fly to Marseille, we had to start by arriving at the airport.

Jerome noticed something was wrong.

"What's bothering you, honey? Did you forget something at home?"

"No, no," I murmured. "Let's go."

I couldn't see myself refusing to take this cab and telling my husband that this was the guy I suspected of having assassinated my Grandma Suzanne. My fear, stemming from my absurd elucubrations, was becoming ridiculous. And it was now quite evident that the real crazy person was in the south of France, where he had kidnapped Sara.

Unless there were several of them?

"Ma'am? If you could get in. We have to get going if you want to be on time at the airport," said the chauffeur politely.

I sat down in the back seat with Jerome. I discreetly sent a text message to my husband, sitting next to me. I felt ridiculous, like I was starring in some poor excuse for a spy movie.

I was sure that it was the same taxi driver who had spoken to me at the funeral, the one who had driven Grandma back to her senior residence, the day before she died.

Jerome's phone vibrated, he read my message and turned his head to me, his eyebrows raised, questioning it.

"So what?" he asked. "What's the problem? Relax, honey. Come here."

He put his arm around my shoulders as the car started up.

I REMAINED silent for a few long minutes, inspecting the roads, examining the signs, fearing that the driver would be taking us elsewhere. Maybe in his hiding place? Like pirates do in movies? *What an idiot I am!* I mentally chastised myself. *Your stories are getting worse and worse, get a grip on it, girl!*

"Are you going on vacation?" the chauffeur asked.

"Not really," I grumbled, trying to cut the discussion off.

"I know, none of my business! It was just a question. But don't we know each other? You're the granddaughter of that poor lady who died not too long ago.

We ran across each other the other day, in Parentis. I remember you. A small world, isn't it!"

"Too small. You're right."

"Once again, so sorry for your loss. Your grandmother seemed like a very nice person."

"She was," I confirmed with a lump in my throat.

I was unable to utter another word until an incident brought me out of my torpidity.

I thought I knew the road leading to the airport quite well, but as we were approaching Bordeaux, I was astonished when our chauffeur left the highway and turned onto a small county road.

"Where are you going?" I asked frankly. "This isn't the road to Merignac Airport."

"Don't worry, my little lady. This is my job, I'm used to it. When traffic starts slowing down before Cestas, it's at a standstill at the bypass. It's quicker to take the sideroads."

And he took so many sideroads that he lost me completely. He took roads I'd never been on, went through little towns I'd never even heard of. I was starting to get a bad feeling about this.

"You're sure of where you're going?"

"You want to catch your plane or not? Just trust me."

How could I trust a guy like that who seemed to be taking us on a ride, both figuratively and literally.

"Let it go, I think he knows what he's doing," Jerome said, trying to reassure me, putting a hand on my thigh.

Now the chauffeur was driving nervously, sometimes hitting the brakes, other times stepping on it and taking the curves on the inside. We were being bounced up and down in the backseat.

I finally was reassured when I saw planes flying in the landing position, a sign we were nearing the airport.

I'd accused that poor chauffeur of being ill-intentioned when all he'd been doing was to get us to the airport on time. He dropped us off, proud of his feat, and wished us a pleasant flight.

It only lasted about an hour. At one thirty, the plane landed on the Marseille-Marignane runway.

Like a baby rocked to sleep by the purring of the motors, hidden behind my sleep mask and oblivious to any noise because of my ear plugs, I finally had fallen asleep. I only woke up when the tires of the plane touched down on the asphalt runway. When I turned my head, I saw that the same thing was true for Jerome, who had simply closed his eyes, no mask needed, with a bit of drool running from the corner of his mouth. My sweetie was handsome when he woke up, despite the bags under his eyes, just as heavy as those in the hold.

The plane taxied up to the gangway. The flight attendants asked us not to get up, not to undo our seat belts, nor turn our phones back on before the plane had completely stopped. As soon as we could, I turned my phone back on and disactivated the airplane mode, a well-named feature here.

It quickly detected a network and the incoming messages, texts, emails, notifications on social media, all that pinged rapidly, too quickly for me to read who was sending them. One of them though immediately attracted my eye.

It had been sent by ***Anonymousemail***.

I swallowed, my throat now dry, and opened the message.

I HOPE you had a good flight to Marignane Airport...

CHAPTER 32
At the last minute

STANDING in the aisle of the plane that had now halted, I jumped when I read that email. And glancing at Jerome's pallid face and wide-open eyes, I was sure he must have received the same one.

"That's impossible," I trembled. "That's impossible."

Then though I realized a harrowing possibility: just a few hours ago, were we really in a taxi taking us to Merignac Airport with the author of that sordid conspiracy? Who else except that chauffeur himself could have known the destination of our impromptu trip, something we'd decided that very morning at the last minute?

Who except for my brother-in-law Damien and Captain Delahousse whom I'd spoken to about our intentions?

Only that taxi driver. The same one who had driven Suzanne on Sunday, who'd walked her right up to her door in her residence. That same one who'd approached me at my grandmother's funeral. Him, still him, him again! He was everywhere, hovering around us, lurking in the shadows.

I HOPE you had a good flight to Marignane Airport...

I'd bet this isn't your honeymoon, is it my little lovebirds? I bet though there are other more exotic and romantic destinations than Marseille for a honeymoon. I would have preferred a more tropical destination. For example, the Caribbean, why not! I think you already know Guadeloupe pretty well. And I'm sure you have great memories of it. Not just great ones though...

But anyway, I don't want to sap your morale with things you'd maybe prefer to forget. Let's look at the present and future.

A very close future.

You're probably hoping to see Sara, Colombe's adorable sister. Please say hi to her from me.

Ah! No, how dumb can I be! That poor lady has been unreachable for days.

Disappeared. Vanished. Pffff!

What was I thinking of? How could you say hi to her from me when you have no idea who I am? Oh! So devious! Excuse me, but I like to play with your nerves, rub salt into your wounds. Some people would even call me sadistic. My grandmother, if she was still here, would call me a naughty boy, those were the most severe words that ever came out of her mouth. May she rest in peace.

But let us return to the matter at hand, or should I say our missing person. Sara, that delicious Sara, who left us, leaving her husband and child just like that. Not a very Christian thing to do!

But anyway, don't bother with me, I know perfectly well where she is our dear missing Sara.

I know or I can guess lots of things. All I need to do is to open up my ears and my eyes. Often you have to know how to read between the lines, to understand what's implied to reach your precious conclusions.

Enough of me blabbing on, I don't want to waste the little time we have left before taking action. Plus it's time for me to have some fun...

Don't forget: the countdown has begun, and the clock is ticking.

See you soon then! I can't wait...

Of course, the message, like the others, wasn't signed. I immediately transferred it to Captain Delahousse, who quickly called me back while we were waiting at the baggage claim.

"Mrs. Bastaro? I just got your message. Did it give you any ideas?"

"I really don't know, but for me everything is just as vague. But I thought I had a good lead. But it doesn't add up."

"Tell me anyway."

So I told him about the suspicions I'd had about the taxi driver. And also how I thought that we'd fallen into a trap. How I saw us as prisoners of that torturer, at his mercy. After that, I had to acknowledge the facts: that taxi driver was just a nice guy. Plus he didn't have the gift of being ubiquitous and couldn't be sequestering Sara in Marseille and driving us to Bordeaux. Or else we were dealing with an organized gang.

"Something we can't exclude," agreed Delahousse. "We'll look into that on our side, our team in Marseille will help us."

"But still," I insisted, "I don't see anyone else than that taxi driver who could have known about our trip. It's like the snake who's biting its own tail!"

"I understand. He can't be here and there at the same time, but still, he was the only one who could have known we were flying from Bordeaux to Marseille."

"Plus he was bragging that he knew where my sister is."

"That could support the hypothesis of a larger organization. One with accomplices. Pay attention when you're in Marseille. Is someone picking you up?"

"Yes. Sara's husband."

"Okay. But make sure you all are careful. Now we have enough elements to open up a real police investigation with all the messages you've received. I'll coordinate the investigators in Marseille, actually I'll be going there this evening or tomorrow morning at the latest."

Finally an upturn, I thought. The cops were now taking us seriously. They understood that we weren't mere players in some asinine role game, but this was in real life.

"Speaking of messages, have you made any progress finding out where they were sent from?"

Captain Delahousse cleared this throat, embarrassed.

"It's complicated," he admitted. "That son of a bitch seems to know his way around a computer. My cyber-investigators are working on it, but so far they haven't found much. The method that guy is using seems to be foolproof, undetectable. They're saying to me that in the hypothesis that they could track down some cyber-lead, it would end up as a cul-de-sac. And at the end of that dead end, they wouldn't even be sure to find the guy we're looking for. But they're on it."

Jerome spotted our suitcase on the conveyor belt and grabbed it while I finished talking to the investigator. We went to the arrivals hall where Damien and innocent little Justine were waiting for us.

"Auntie Colombe!" she shouted out as I walked through the sliding doors.

She jumped out of her father's arm to hop into mine. I hugged her tightly, I needed — even maybe more than her — some cuddles. I knew that she ignored the reason for our visit and forced myself not to burst into tears thinking about her mother — my sister, the person I grew up next to when I was Justine's age.

. . .

In the car, while we were speeding towards Rousset, neither Jerome, Damien nor I could find the strength to carry on a conversation, except to exchange a few insipid banalities. We didn't even mention our wedding, I knew I wouldn't be able to take it. Luckily for us, Justine, as usual, talked for all four of us. A real chatterbox, something that did us a world of good.

Made us forget, for a few fleeting moments, our situation.

Forget Sara? Of course not, that would have been impossible. Her image was continuously floating in front of my eyes.

Where was she right now?

Was she still alive at least?

Were we making a mistake by going to Marseille? After all, though she'd been kidnapped there, there was no proof that she still was in that city.

Where are you Sara?

CHAPTER 33
Reddening and traces

SHE HAD DOZED off once again. Undoubtedly the effects of the narcotic she'd been administered, unless it was simply an excess from that bottle of rum she saw when she woke up, lying on the wooden floor next to the bed.

Her wrists and ankles hurt each time she tried to change her position on the mattress. That was the price to be paid, that was her punishment, something she was aware of and accepted.

The door of that room opened again, squeaking on its poorly oiled hinges.

The face of a man was visible on the doorstep. A face with harsh and closed features. Above that authoritarian face, there was a peaked cap with a svastika on it, like the ones that German officers in the army wore during the Second World War, an impression that was confirmed by the uniform the tall, blond man was wearing. The sound of his leather boots resonated on the hardwood floor as he advanced towards the bed where Sara, nude, was lying.

"Finally awake I see!" he murmured, taking the gag from the young lady's mouth. "You're going to be a nice girl, aren't you?"

He pronounced those words while whipping a riding crop in the palm of his leather gloved hand.

"Please," Sara stammered. "No!"

The man sneered almost like a hysterical hyena.

"Because you think you're the one who's deciding things now?"

"Please, untie me, I'm begging you."

"Maybe... after. If you're a good girl. If you don't scream too much, for example."

The pseudo neo-Nazi leaned towards the bed and suddenly ripped that thin sheet off that was partially covering the young lady. Sara's skin immediately had goosebumps. From the cold? Fear? Shame? A mixture of all of the above?

The man's right hand advanced towards the bed. He touched the young lady's breast with the tip of his riding crop. Delicately, using little circular movements, he played with her nipple, a nipple that perked little by little under the effect of the object's cold touch. Sara clenched her teeth and closed her eyes.

The man then ran the endpiece of his crop along Sara's stomach, with slow movements, as if he was drawing an invisible arabesque on her white skin. He went around her blond pubis, and Sara squeezed her legs together.

"Stop that!" he barked.

After a moment of hesitation, she obediently obeyed him and relaxed her legs. The riding crop started up again, going down on the side of her thigh to her ankle, which was stretched by the cloth tying it to the foot of the bed, back up the other leg until it reached the spot that the French painter Courbet had magnified and glorified in his painting *The Origin of the World*. Sara suppressed a scream. The man's authoritarian look ordered her to be silent and submissive. Plus his clothing naturally strengthened his authority.

The endpiece of the riding crop slid onto the young lady's quivering vulva, trying to force its way in.

"Please, no, not that," Sara begged.

"Who's in charge here?" the uniformed man said with a loud voice. "I'll detach your legs. You promise to be good?"

The young lady was silent, terrified.

"I didn't hear anything! Answer me! You'll be good if I untie you?"

"Yes."

The fake Nazi untied Sara's ankles, and she immediately felt relieved. She felt like rubbing her aching skin, but as her arms were still tied to the headboard, this was impossible for her.

"Turn around!" ordered the fake officer.

"I can't."

"Excuse me? Are you refusing? Do you want me to get mad?"

"I'm aching all over, I can't even move..."

"*Tsk, tsk, tsk*, we'll see about that."

He put his riding crop down on the mattress and grabbed her left ankle, and with a circular movement, pushed it towards the other side of the bed. Her hips turned as he tipped her onto her stomach. Spending hours lying on her back had numbed her entire body. Now her face was against the mattress, her arms crossed above her head, her buttocks open to the riding crop, she was at the complete mercy of that man leaning down over her.

And indeed, the man touched Sara's buttocks with the endpiece of the object, one that experienced riders call a *claquette*. She shivered and her gluteus muscles unintentionally contracted when he lightly whipped her with it. She was tempted to shout, but contained herself, remembering what her torturer had said.

Then moderate blows continued, on both of her buttocks. She could feel the heat rising little by little, announcing both reddening and traces.

"Stop! Please, stop!"

"You're right," agreed the man, putting an end to his sadistic little game.

He paused, saying nothing. Sara with her face in the mattress couldn't see what was taking place behind her back. All she could hear was the sound of a metal buckle being unbuckled, the noise of pants falling to the ground, and the clinking of the buckle on the wooden floor. A few seconds later, she could feel the weight of the man on the mattress between her spread legs.

She had a good idea of what would follow with a mixture of fear and lust, mixed feelings that she was having trouble dissimilating. When the man penetrated her without a word, she bit the pillow and didn't move, enduring the act until the man finally collapsed heavily on her.

They remained that way for several long minutes, silent, both of them buried in their bleak thoughts. Then the man pulled out, leaving her panting.

"You had enough?"

Hot tears were falling on Sara's cheeks, moistening the sheet. She swallowed painfully because of her dry thirsty throat.

"Please… I don't want to play anymore."

CHAPTER 34
A premeditated act

FOR HOURS on end the investigators from the station in Marseille analyzed the footage from the surveillance cameras that the company managing the Mucem Museum parking lot had given them. Black and white images, of a mediocre quality, allowed them to visualize all the vehicles, as the cameras were located at the entrance and exit of the lot. There were others though, in each corner of the four floors, as well as in the stairwell and in the elevators. And one more focusing on the automated payment machines. That way the operators could see in real time the entire parking lot, one used by thousands of cars throughout the day and night.

Luckily for them, thanks to the license plate on Sara's Kadjar, the investigators were able to localize their research in a very precise timeframe. At least they knew that the license plate had been photographed by one of the cameras, located at the height of those plates, where you take your parking ticket, exactly at 3:36 pm.

But it never left.

They'd ruined their eyes looking at the footage to try to find the vehicle on each of the floors she'd driven through, up until she parked on the third sublevel. They were able to distinguish a silhouette walking from the car, getting into the elevator and going upstairs until she disappeared in the streets of Marseille.

The investigators had to watch several hours of the following footage, looking for any suspicious elements. What they were searching for was the presence of the eventual author of her kidnapping.

Finally one of the policemen saw Sara at 6:39 pm, when she walked back into the lot, by the automated payment machines. That corroborated with what Malika had told them, that friend she'd spent the afternoon with. But though Sara did stop in front of the machine, she curiously took her credit card out of her wallet before putting it back in again without paying.

It though was possible to pay with a credit card upon leaving, one of the investigators said. She was probably going to pay that way.

Except that her car never budged from the third sublevel.

A few minutes later, on that same floor, they saw Sara's silhouette coming out of the elevator and walking towards her vehicle. Then going in.

She remained there for a few minutes. The investigators couldn't see inside the car, but according to the footage, they didn't see her leave.

"Unless we missed her..." said one of the police officers.

The cameras upstairs weren't still images and swept across the parking lot in order to film the entire floor, which cut down on the number of cameras required. That technical and economic advantage became a drawback when you were trying to concentrate on only one given point. That made it completely possible for the young lady to have left her car while the camera was filming another zone.

That probably wasn't the case though, as about ten minutes later, they all noticed something.

With his back to the camera, a man was standing next to the Kadjar, right next to the front door on the driver's side. He was tall, quite slim, and had a cap on that dissimulated his face.

But though the file had a mediocre resolution, the policemen could see the man pounding on the glass of the vehicle's window before trying unsuccessfully to open the door. It was minute, but when zooming in, it was clear. They could see a young lady sitting in the driver's seat.

Then the car door opened, and Sara Lesueur got out, slightly hidden by the stature of the man, who moved to let her exit.

"She's got her purse on her shoulder," said one of the cops looking at the footage.

"And she closed the door, but we didn't see the

lights blink, like they would have had she locked the car."

"They seem to know each other…"

"Totally, she doesn't seem to be afraid, otherwise she never would have got out of the car."

"Look! They're leaving together, heading for the stairs."

"As if they'd decided to meet up in that parking lot."

"Except that we never got to see that guy's face, on any of the cameras," regretted one of the policemen.

"Wait a sec, shift over to the camera in the stairwell."

They saw two silhouettes on those images, but once again, only the man's back as he was walking towards the stairs, and his face was hidden by his cap.

"A pro! He knows he's being filmed and where the cameras are. He must have done his homework."

"A premeditated act."

"Organized between her and him! Just a sec, go back. Right there. Look, they're not exiting the parking lot on foot, they're leaving the stairs on the first floor underground. Switch cameras. Match it to the -1 level at the same minute as the one on the stairs."

The police officers found the couple walking side by side towards a car parked on that floor. The lights were blinking, signaling that the car was being opened remotely, a light Toyota sedan, if you could trust the black and white footage.

Two people got in, the man in the driver's seat, and

she got in the passenger seat. The car backed up, turned and took the exit ramp.

"Switch to the exit camera! Same time!"

The Toyota stopped at the payment terminal, the driver opened his window, and an arm emerged to insert the ticket. At the same time another camera filmed the license plate, which the investigators immediately noted.

All they had to do now was to consult the license plate registrations file to find out who the owner of that vehicle was, the one that was driving Sara Lesueur to an unknown destination.

CHAPTER 35
Fear pegged to our hearts

MY LITTLE NIECE Justine had gone to bed and was already sleeping. Damien, Jerome and I, helpless and dejected, were in my sister's living room and her cruel absence was eating away at us beyond anything we could have imagined.

"It's been over twenty-four hours now without any news from her," Damien lamented with a voice muffled by anxiety.

I also noticed though that his voice was slurred by all the alcohol he'd ingurgitated that evening. His way of drowning his sorrows.

We hadn't wanted to withdraw the possibility for him to forget the events of these last hours for a while. And I had to admit that I also, despondent by my sister's disappearance, had downed a couple of glasses of rum between two sessions of tears. What dominated our rare discussions was incomprehension, mixed with the fear that she was already dead. Fear was pegged to our hearts, we weren't expecting any good news. But still, perhaps we would have preferred to have known what had happened to Sara, rather than that silence, doubt and ignorance. Isn't ignorance one of the worst tortures?

For dinner, because we still had to eat, we ordered a couple of pizzas that Justine, unaware of the situation, gobbled down, while we found it hard to swallow anything.

"I still don't understand what could have happened," repeated Damien for the umpteenth time while shaking his head and pouring himself another glass of rum. "Why isn't she answering?"

He couldn't even count the number of times he'd called her, with her voice-mail message invariably answering. At first, he'd left her messages, then he got tired of always repeating the same words, the same cries of anxiety and apprehension, the same electronic silences. He now was hanging up as soon as he'd heard Sara's voice repeating her welcome message. Hearing her without being able to touch her was breaking his heart.

Then his phone rang. He rushed to it, tipping the little table over with our half-empty glasses on it, hoping that it finally was her!

But he frowned when he saw the number.

Unknown caller.

At least someone who wasn't on his contact list.

"Hello," he stammered.

"Captain Vincent Delahousse. I'm overseeing the

investigation about your wife's disappearance as well as the one that your sister-in-law and brother-in-law contacted me about."

"Did you find her? Is she okay?"

He suddenly had a minute glimmer of hope.

"No, I'm sorry, we're not there yet, but we do have a serious lead to investigate. Mr. Lesueur, I've got a delicate question I have to ask…"

"At this point… I don't think anything could hurt me."

"Mr. Lesueur, I apologize for asking this, but lately, has the relationship with your wife been normal? Has your couple been having some problems?"

"Excuse me? I don't understand what a question about our couple has to do with anything, Captain. Stuff like that is private," continued Damien, turning towards us with a worried look in his eyes. "My wife was kidnapped by some sadistic person who announced what he'd be doing to my sister-in-law and brother-in-law. That seems clear to me, don't you agree?"

The policeman cleared this throat, but as a professional, he continued.

"No, actually it's not as clear as that really. As you're not making this easy for me, I'm going to have to be direct with you. Mr. Lesueur, to the best of your knowledge, did your wife have a lover?"

. . .

From where I was sitting, I couldn't hear what Captain Delahousse had said, but when I looked at Damien's face his jaw had dropped open, and he remained silent. I could see that their interview wasn't going well.

"Let me put it in other words, Mr. Lesueur. Was your wife having an affair with another man?"

"I have no idea," whispered my brother-in-law, sitting down. "Not that I know of."

"Okay. Then have you ever heard of someone named Erich Elstrom?"

Now it was his eyes popping wide open.

"Could you say that again?"

"Erich Elstrom."

"No, never heard of him. Why?"

"Because to be transparent with you, Mr. Lesueur, we were able to watch the camera footage of the Mucem parking lot where you wife parked her car. And she doesn't seem to have been kidnapped..."

"What? So she's alright then..."

"At this stage of the investigation, I can't guarantee that," Delahousse regretted.

"Well, why isn't she answering me then?"

"I can't tell you that either, but her cell phone can't be tracked, unfortunately. And believe me, that would really help us there."

"So who is that guy then?" asked my brother-in-law, now irritated. "And where the hell did you get that name from?"

"Like I said, we were able to retrace the last

minutes of where your wife was using the surveillance cameras in the parking lot. She met a man on the third sublevel of the Mucem lot and left her car there, without even locking it. Then, without visibly being forced by that man, they left together in his car, a Toyota, and we've got its license plate. And according to its plate, the car belongs to someone named Erich Elstrom, though we can't affirm that he was the person in the car. We couldn't see his face. So, you continue to say that you've never heard of that name and you're sure that your wife isn't having an affair?"

"I have never heard that name in my life. As for an affair, I'm not denying it. I simply don't know."

"Could it be a friend of hers? A colleague? Someone she works with? Think about it. And if you remember anything, call me immediately, okay?"

"Of course. But, with that name, can you find out where my wife is? That *Elstrom* must live someplace."

"Of course he does, and we already have tried to find them at his latest known address. But had we found them, I would have told you right away. His house was empty."

Damien hung up, putting his phone in his back pocket.

"Have you guys ever heard of an *Erich Elstrom*?"

"We should have?" asked Jerome.

CHAPTER 36
Like a whirlwind

Summer 2008

WHAT HE HAD BEEN FEARING *for months was happening right under his bloodshot eyes.*

He clenched his fists with wrath, hatred, and disgust too.

Had they thought they were being discreet, those bastards had their fingers burned. He saw them trying to sneak away on that good-looking kid's Vespa, that kid who had the best scooter, the trendiest one, the one who attracted girls like there was no tomorrow. A scooter like that was like a fishing net for chicks.

Unless of course he himself was the chick magnet, with or without his Vespa. All he had to do was crack one of those Crest toothpaste smiles, run his fingers through his blond wavy hair, look at one of those broads with his blue eyes and that was it! No sooner said than done! Hop on my beauty, let me take you for a ride to heaven.

Fuck! Life sure isn't fair. It's easy to see that everyone isn't born with the same chances, as if life were a mere and huge game of roulette in a casino. Some people's bets play out, whereas others always lose. Others bet on the white pocket, the one that pays the most. That son of a bitch must be unique, have Lady Luck eating out of his hand.

He though, has the feeling that his ball had literally been ejected from the roulette wheel when he was born. Bing! No more betting. And during his whole life, he tried his utmost to get back in the game. To keep on playing, to insist, one of these days his number would come up.

All you had to do was to persist.

Now though, he saw them leave on their scooter and quickly hopped on his own, a second-hand moped that his parents got him, saying that it would be sufficient, that he certainly didn't need a two-wheeled Ferrari to waste gas in the village. What they didn't understand, his parents, was that he didn't want to screw around in the village, but just to ride on a chick bait bike. Seeing as he couldn't count on his physical attributes, what he wanted to do was to seduce the girls differently, materially.

But that wasn't going to happen either.

The blond guy's *scooter started up like a whirlwind, with a girl sitting behind him, her arms hugging that asshole's waist, her head leaning on his back. They quickly drove away from him.*

His advantage? They had no idea he was there. He was good at hiding, at being invisible, he'd always been. Ever since he turned thirteen, he'd developed stunning camouflage techniques. As the girls he was interested in never noticed him, he knew how to make himself forgotten. He was so terribly ordinary.

He followed them from afar, making sure they could never see him in the rear-view mirror of their colorful scooter. Anyway, they had loads of other things to do, those two lovebirds, rather than looking behind. All they were thinking of was getting away from everyone as quickly as possible to do their dirty deeds in some isolated place; he wasn't born yesterday. He knew that they had been flirting with each other for a while. She had finally caved and let herself be seduced by that beefcake.

A beefcake, that was the right word. A hunk of beef, mouthwatering. Nice to look at, that was it. The opposite of himself. Maybe that was the problem with that age: gals dreamed when they looked at those funhouse mirrors. All the guys needed was to have a few muscles under their wifebeaters, to have a good-sized lump in front of their drawers, and gel on their hair.

He didn't have any of that. But one day he'd get even with them. As years went by, the girls would finally understand and appreciate his inner beauty, his humor, his brains.

For now though, they seemed to prefer the mirages of

external beauty, like the one hanging onto that beefcake on the back of his scooter.

They'd left the village, rushing towards the plains. The two-wheeled vehicle suddenly turned toward the right, taking a path that led to a distant forest, one that was at least two miles from any houses. They were looking for a place where no one would see them doing their dirty deeds.

He had to, though he didn't want to.

He turned his moped off and laid it down in the ditch. He'd walk there so they wouldn't hear those infernal noises his bike made.

He knew only too well how to be discreet. He could have been nicknamed 'Stealth Mode Guy.' Or 'Peeping Tom', if they chose to abhor rather than admire his talents of making himself oblivious. He quietly walked up to the fringe of the forest. He could hear them snickering, chuckling. He got even closer, as carefully as possible, avoiding stepping on the branches that could crack below his soles. He now was kneeling, making himself as small as possible, invisible. He was near their scooter, and for a fleeting moment he wanted to plunge his pocketknife into its wheels and get the hell out of there.

But his desire to see them was stronger. He had to surprise them, why not take a couple of pics, that could be a good souvenir.

They thought they were alone, it was nearly pitiful watching them. Had they only known that his perverted eyes were spying on them behind the bushes.

Instead of that, they were loving the moment, those

lovebirds with their forbidden love. They were kissing each other on the mouth, using their tongues, as if they wanted to make up for all the time they'd lost. Years of unsatisfied lust. Years of hanging around each other without touching. Now that they'd taken the first step, they were devouring each other.

And in his hiding place, he witnessed it all. Though he suffered from being a mere spectator. He was burning with desire to take that beefcake's place and hold that beautiful girl in his own arms, the girl he'd desired for so many years.

That girl he was gazing at looked just like the one in his dreams, the one in his moist fantasies below his covers each night when he was thinking of her.

Her, the one that bastard was making out with and slipping his hands under her t-shirt to find her tiny and pert little breasts. She let him do that while moaning, leaning her head sideways, her eyes closed, her mouth half open. She seemed to be liking that, that little b... No! He couldn't think of her like that, she deserved something better. Though... Though she was allowing herself to be petted by someone else, not him. That asshole's fingers were playing with her nipples while he was kissing her neck.

And she allowed him to continue.

Hidden behind the bushes, he had his hand on his pants, on his budding erection, there where it hurts.

The other guy dared to go even farther, taking advantage of the young girl's apparent permission. She'd agreed, he was going to seize the opportunity. His hand moved between her legs, onto her moist and warm shorts.

There though she suddenly reared back, pushing him away. He insisted, she pulled back. Sat up, followed by him. She put her head between her hands, and he began to profusely apologize. She began to cry, said she wanted to go home, that they shouldn't have, that they didn't have the right to. He disagreed, she protested. He finally gave in.

They both walked up to the scooter, passing way too near to the one hidden in the bushes. He nearly felt like jumping out of his hiding place just like a Jack-in-the-Box, scaring them, socking the guy in his handsome face, clocking him in that face he was so jealous of.

But he didn't, he even held his breath. Then he took a couple more photos that could always be useful to him... later.

Revenge is a dish best served cold, at least that's how the old saying goes.

CHAPTER 37
An adrenaline rush

THE COUPLE HAD their arms around each other on the bed. The young lady was crying softly, sobbing in the powerful arms of that blond man who seemed unable to appease her.

"I really screwed up here," said Sara while hiding her head in Erich's hairy chest. "I don't know why I did something like this. I made a mistake. I cheated on him. I cheated on you. Everyone made a mistake!"

"Stop torturing yourself, we already talked about all of this, you're not going to regret it today."

Sara pushed her lover's arms away, got up and picked up her clothing that had been scattered all over the floor.

"I don't know. I don't know anymore. I have to think about my daughter. If only for her, I should have thought this over before going missing like this."

The young lady took her phone out of her bag that was hanging on a hook on the door. For her selfish pleasure, and only for that, she had wanted to abandon everyone and everything. Just for a few days, a few hours, just to forget everything. To unchain that fire that had been smoldering her for such a long time, one that she wasn't able to liberate and put out with her husband.

"Do you have a charger?"

"Yes. My phone is plugged in over there."

The adulterous woman plugged her phone in, and the screen lit up. She unlocked it and let the phone slowly wake up while she slowly put her clothes on. With over twenty-four hours of an uncharged battery, the cell phone seemed just as numb as she was, still feeling the bite of the bonds she'd had around her ankles and wrists.

She felt Erich's presence behind her back and turned around. He dominated her by his height, his wide shoulders, his nude chest that accentuated his pumped muscles. He intrinsically was a good-looking man, with a charismatic charm. As soon as she'd set eyes on him for the first time, his light blue eyes had plunged right to the depths of Sara's soul. His Scandinavian features made her crazy about him. His chiseled body, his powerful arms, in a nutshell: his status as a dominant male made her want to surrender herself to all his desires.

His desires that her own desires quickly responded to and matched. She was bored in her daily life, stuck in a monotonous routine, and had drifted off in a turbulent ocean until she got swallowed up in its abysses. Dark depths where violence was desired, sought, shared, then assumed.

Both of them were consenting adults. No crimes had been committed. Zero constraints, just pleasure. A pleasure born from sweet physical pain that led to a pure adrenaline rush. That molecule that had survived through the ages, that neurotransmitter that prehistorical men generated when a ferocious animal was rushing towards them and that made them flee to escape death. Of course, neither Sara nor Erich lived in the Stone Age, but their staged meetings allowed them to increase their desires tenfold, to multiply their pleasure and nearly always reach a concomitant orgasm.

After that though their tension dropped. Especially for Sara, who, when their lovemaking was over, invariably felt ashamed and disgusted with herself. She'd leave those secret rendezvous with the conviction that in the future she'd never give in again, and when she'd go back home, she needed quite a while to feel clean again, in her soul much more than her body. She'd try to get closer to Damien, to hold onto the buoys of his life: his leisure activities, his daughter, his work and his friends.

Quickly though she would become bored once again. Sometimes she was the one contacting Erich, other times he was the one harassing her with messages when she was at work. They'd always end up meeting each other in the third sublevel of the Mucem Museum's parking lot and would leave in the man's Toyota towards their secret hiding place, their private den of their unholy and unspeakable pleasures.

They'd drink and smoke a few illicit substances that would help the young lady free herself completely from her psychological manacles and her Christian stranglehold.

They'd draw up a scenario together, each time a different one. That was always so much fun. Last night she was the one who'd asked him to wear a Nazi uniform, who knows why! The uniform, its power, his male authority, her obeying and fearing him, her total submission, all of that put together had led her towards an intangible elsewhere.

"Take me back," whispered Sara to Erich, who had put on his everyday clothes. He had folded up the Nazi uniform and put it back in the box take it back to that shop they both went to.

"No!"

A brief and scathing answer.

"Excuse me?" asked Sara, astonished.

"I'm not taking you back. You're not leaving. You're staying here with me."

"Erich... I'm so sorry, I thought this over. I know that this is hard for you to hear, but we both said this. Our love story wasn't going to be one that would last."

"Shut up!"

The words bounced off the walls in that empty room just as loudly as the sounds of that riding crop on the young lady's buttocks a few hours earlier. The words though hurt more than the leather did.

"What? Oh! Don't talk to me like that, Erich. We're no longer playing. It's over. You're not wearing that uniform now, you're Erich Elstrom."

The man walked up to the young lady, dominating her by his height.

"I'm sick and tired of being your toy boy, staying in the shadows all the time. I don't want you to leave like that anymore, going home to find your nice little doggie of a husband."

"You don't understand anything, I don't want to see my husband, I want to see my daughter."

"Too late. You should have thought about that earlier. You had months to think things over. And now that I've got you, I'm not going to let you go."

He grabbed Sara's arm firmly and she began to struggle.

"Let go of me!"

"I said *no*, are you deaf or what?"

Their faces were nearly touching now. Sara could smell Erich's alcohol-filled breath. He must have kept on drinking while she was passed out on the bed. Too much alcohol certainly explained his unusual behavior. Whatever the reason, the young lady was beginning to fear her lover. This was the very first time he had been aggressive outside of their agreed upon and totally assumed sexual scenarios. In a movement he hadn't been expecting, she got out of his grip and rushed to her phone.

She wanted to flee, run out of that little house while trying to make a phone call. But she had time to do neither. Swooping down on her, and with his wide palm, Erich hit her phone which flew out of her hands. It flew up into the air before bouncing against the wall, where it fell apart, with pieces falling here and there on the floor.

Sara began to shout.

"No one's gonna hear you here! That was one of the reasons we chose this hiding place, wasn't it? To live our love with discretion and intimacy... So just shut up now Sara!"

Erich voice was getting louder and louder and he literally bellowed out her first name. At the same time, he'd moved in front of her to prevent her from leaving.

"Let me out of here, you're scaring me now"

"You... are gonna... stay!"

"Erich, you had too much to drink, you don't know what you're saying nor what you're doing. Come here, lie down a little, you'll feel better after that."

"Don't try to play any tricks on me. I know what I want. And it's you!"

Erich finally controlled Sara and lifted her up, carrying her in his arms towards "the torture room," as they called it between themselves, though she was kicking, trying to get away from him and screaming at him to let her go.

All of that noise and shouting had isolated them from outside and they didn't hear the footsteps nearing the cottage.

They also missed the slight creaking of the front door that Sara had unlocked when she was trying to flee, as it opened.

Caught up in their fury, they didn't see a silhouette sneaking up on them from behind.

Nor did they notice that baseball bat before it swung in the air.

CHAPTER 38
A good alibi

"I CAN'T DENY that sometimes I'd thought that Sara was cheating on me," Damien finally admitted, after having downed an umpteenth glass of rum. "I did cross my mind, she was often so terrible distant from me. Very cold. She wouldn't let me touch her. As if she was disgusted by me even."

I put my hand on my brother-in-law's arm.

"You don't have to give us any details you know."

The living room was dimly lit up, conducive to telling secrets. Justine had been asleep in her room for three hours now, not knowing how tormented her father was. He continued.

"Some evenings, when I'd go to bed, I had the feeling that Sara had been crying. I'd take her in my arms, she wouldn't turn around, but that did seem to calm her. And in the morning when I'd ask her what the matter was, she invariably answered that she was fine. But the rubber band holding us together was stretching more every day, ready to snap. With hindsight, I now can reinterpret some of her words and actions from a different angle. Now that I know..."

Damien paused, looking out at nothing, his glass in his hand. At the end of the hall, in that sudden silence, I thought I heard Justine moan while she was sleeping. Poor kid, her mother's absence was hard on her, especially at night. Her father continued.

"The past couple of months she'd been gone much more than usual, especially with her friend, Malika. At least that was what she told me. Now I think she was just a good alibi. Sometimes she was gone all day and only got home late at night. Plus a couple of times she stayed overnight."

"You didn't think that was strange?" Jerome scratched his head with a crooked smile.

Damien shook his head.

"She told me she had meetings in Paris, at the head office. And now I realize I was stupid enough to believe her."

"Maybe that was true. You're interpreting that from a different point of view, but you don't have any proof."

"Proof she was cheating on me? No, I don't, just a vague feeling that seems to be true now."

Deep down inside, those words, *cheating on me*, gave me heartburn as I remembered my wedding vows, just a week ago in that church in Biscarrosse. *I promise to be faithful to you, in good times and in bad, in sickness and in health, and to love you all the days of my life...* Wishful thinking! But we were all mere humans, at the end of the day... Humans and thus fallible.

We suddenly heard a scream.

"Mommy! Mommy! Mommy!" screamed Justine from her room, with a broken voice, interrupted by sobs and hiccups. Damien ran to her bedside, followed by Jerome and me.

The little girl was sitting cross-legged on her bed, her eyes nearly closed, as if she was having a nightmare while awake, or a terrifying sleepwalking episode.

"Sweetie, everything's okay. Daddy's here. Shh."

While running his fingers through her hair, Damien was whispering to his daughter and kissing her. The little girl woke up completely.

"I dreamed that mommy was dead."

I interpreted that sentence as a bad omen, fearing that the little girl had some sort of telepathy with her mother. I couldn't get that out of my head.

Then Damien's phone in the living room rang. He didn't pick up, busy trying to calm his little daughter down so she'd go back to sleep, which she did about ten minutes later. At her age, cuddling with one of her parents was like a magical potion.

When Damien got back to the living room, he opened his voicemail and his voice broke down.

"The cops just located Sara's phone."

It was as if the wall of silence that had been weighing

down our hearts since last night had flown away, and we were hopeful.

Our eyes began to twinkle with a new glint and finally Jerome and I both smiled frankly.

A smile quickly put out by our brother-in-law's words.

"I have to call Captain Delahousse back right away. He finished his message by warning me. They still haven't found her. Neither dead nor alive."

CHAPTER 39
The silent eye in the sky

A BIT EARLIER, not too far from the Lesueur's home, the squad in charge of the investigation, headed by Captain Delahousse, had suddenly perked up.

"Cap? I think that Sara Lesueur's cell phone has suddenly come back to life."

All the team members gathered around the police officer in charge of monitoring Sara Lesueur's and Erich Elstrom's phone activity, believing that as he owned that Toyota parked in the Mucem lot, he probably was her kidnapper.

A bit earlier, as they had registered Sara Lesueur in the missing persons file, the investigators had been authorized to access her phone records, meaning the monthly detailed invoices that the telecom companies sent out to their clients. They gave the details of phone calls made and received, whether they were messages or actual calls. They thus were able to determine with certainty that Sara was planning on meeting up with

Erich Elstrom. His phone number had popped up often in the list of numbers called and messages the young lady had sent, including and especially on the day that she went missing. That for them seemed to prove that her kidnapping was actually a romantic getaway.

This though, was more of a deduction than true proof, as the records did not give them any content of the messages, only the number calling or called, at what time it took place and its duration. The same thing was true for any text messages. Knowing what was actually being said or written would only have been possible only if there was a type of spyware installed on her phone.

All of that explained the voluntary disappearance of the young lady, but didn't give them any clues about where she now was. It was impossible to geolocalize her phone, as the battery was empty, the phone of course was mute. The same thing was true for Erich Elstrom's phone, though they believed that he had probably disabled the geolocalization function in it.

Except that while the young lady had been missing for over twenty-four hours, her phone had suddenly woken up. The satellites had immediately located it.

"So where is she?" asked Delahousse impatiently.

The police officer in front of his computer screen clicked on a link and Google Maps opened up in a new tab. First there was a map of all of France, then very quickly, the zoom was activated, searching for the exact position of the phone number. That virtual map of

France began to expand, zooming in on its southeastern part at first, and then in the PACA Region. Leaving Marseille and the Mediterranean behind, that eye of the spy in the sky slid over to the Alps and then quickly focused on the Verdon Natural Regional Park, only displaying zones of grass and cliffs, with the Segries Monastery in red right in the middle. Then its focal lens slowed down and zoomed in on a dense forest, with a few white rural roads winding around lazily not too far from the ravines which were in blue. There, at the end of a path ending in a cul-de-sac, the pointer began to blink, indicating the exact position of Sara Lesueur's phone.

"She's there!" exclaimed the police officer proudly, as if he himself had found her at the end of a long treasure hunt in the mountains of this rural area. "Not far from Saint-Jurs."

Delahousse leaned down to look at the screen, trying to see how to reach that point.

"There's nothing here!" he complained.

The place the geolocalization system had targeted seemed to be in the middle of nowhere, about three thousand feet high, between ravines and dense forests.

As if Sara — or who knows, maybe just her phone — had parachuted out of a plane and landed there.

"How far is it?" asked Delahousse.

"Two good hours at least, if we don't have any problems."

"We gotta get going then."

CHAPTER 40
Abdicating

THE UNMARKED CAR was driving north on the A51. Luckily traffic wasn't dense when they'd left Marseille and as soon as the policemen turned off of the A7 heading towards Septemes-les-Vallons, the double highway was clear. The car sped quickly down the highway, with its flashing lights though they hadn't turned the siren on. A dark and moonless night, unsettling.

The silence in the car was suddenly interrupted by one of the policemen sitting in the back.

"Cap? We've got a problem."

"Now what?" asked Delahousse.

"We lost the signal!"

The police officer handed him his computer on which he was following Sara Lesueur's phone. The blinker cursor in the region of Saint-Jurs was gone.

"All of a sudden like that?"

"Yes."

Since they'd the signal had gone live, it had never moved. And then suddenly, nothing.

"What does that mean? Maybe we have to reboot? Actualize the page? Got me, but it's probably a connection issue or a bug in the program."

"I already tried, Cap. That didn't do anything. There's no longer any signal."

Delahousse was sitting in the passenger's seat.

"How long till we get there?" he asked the driver.

"I'd say forty-five minutes at the most."

"Step on it!"

⁓

Ten minutes later, the captain's phone rang. It was Damien Lesueur.

"Where's my wife?" he asked pointblank.

"It looks like she's in the Verdon Park someplace."

"What do you mean *it looks like*?"

"Because we're driving to the place where her phone last went live."

"Last? What about now?"

"We lost the signal. Probably some technical glitch," the policeman said to reassure him. "I'll call you back as soon as we know more. But, by any chance, does the Verdon Natural Regional Park ring a bell for you? Do you have a cottage there? A chalet in the mountains? Have you gone there on vacation?"

"None of the above, why? Just tell me where my wife is. I want to go get her."

"No way! You just calm down and keep your phone on, that'll help us more. I'll call you back as soon as I know anything, okay?"

All Damien could do was to abdicate as the cop had already hung up.

∼

Fearing that the signal would quickly disappear, the investigators had of course noted the exact GSP location and had put it into their vehicle's SATNAV device. Better to be safe than sorry. After having left the tollway, they continued on the D6, then the D8, the D953 and finally the D108. Right before arriving in the little town of Saint-Jurs, they had to take unnamed roads, making them think they'd soon be driving on quite impracticable ones. They luckily had taken a four-wheel drive — following Erich Elstrom's example with his Toyota Hilux — and were able to drive down those pot-holed paths, ones that normal cars wouldn't have been able to drive on. A wise precaution, though their car wasn't as well adapted as Sara's lover's pickup.

Luck wasn't on their side that dark night and it had begun to rain in the mountains. A huge downpour with drops coming off the foliage the cops were driving under, falling on their roof with an annoying staccato.

"That's all we needed," Delahousse railed.

"Only another mile and a half," the chauffeur reassured him. "But they won't be the easiest ones, I'm afraid."

As if it had heard what he'd said, though he was driving slowly, the vehicle's back tires slid on the loose soil. The driver immediately put it into four-wheel drive mode.

Fifteen minutes later, they heard their SATNAV's mechanical voice.

"*You have arrived at your destination.*"

Some useless info from the software as the policemen all saw after they'd turned down the last curve, a little wooden cabin in the cul-de-sac.

With Erich Elstrom's Toyota parked right in front.

There were lights on inside coming through one of the windows in the back of the cabin.

THE DRIVER TURNED the car off and Delahousse was the first one to open his door.

"Let's stay in a group and be careful," he warned them.

The four men got out of the vehicle and closed the car doors gently. A gust of water-filled wind hammered them right in the face.

Delahousse and his colleagues all checked their service weapons and made sure everyone was wearing their bulletproof vests.

The captain took the lead to the cabin's front door,

which was sheltered by a porch. You could say that the rain here was their ally; no one in the cabin could hear their footsteps nor the car's motor when they were arriving.

The captain put his ear to the door. There was no noise inside. Yet, seeing how the Toyota was parked in front of the cottage, and it was pitch black and pouring rain, he was pretty sure that the adulterous couple weren't taking a stroll outside. Or perhaps they were sleeping, exhausted after having made love?

He turned the doorknob, the door opened easily, and he pushed it completely open with his left shoulder, his gun in front of him. The first room, that only had a table with four chairs around it, didn't have any lights on. On the other hand, there was light filtering from below the door of the next room. The four men broke up, each one examining one of the four walls, though paying attention to the door at the back of the room that was slightly ajar. Suddenly one of them stepped on something that crackled under his heavy boots, with a sharp noise.

"Shit! What the hell?"

He leaned down and picked up the pieces of what seemed to him to be a broken cell phone.

"I think you found the signal again," Delahousse whispered ironically before going up to the door leading to the room with the light on, but in which there was a deathly silence.

All four were close to each other and the captain kicked the door open.

...

They witnessed as strange scene: a tall blond man was lying nude on the bed, his arms and legs attached to the bed by scarves and handcuffs, a gag on his mouth.

CHAPTER 41
Influence and hold

THE MAN WAS VISIBLY UNCONSCIOUS. The hematomas on his temple as well as the dried blood on his cheek proved that he'd been the victim of a violent act. The investigators' report would include the given formula: *a blow from a blunt object*. An object they hadn't been able to find.

And they hadn't been able to find Sara Lesueur either, though they of course picked up her phone and placed it in an evidence bag for future analysis. They'd believed at first that the young lady had been kidnapped, then they suspected that she simply ran off with her lover to this cottage in the middle of the Verdon Natural Regional Park, meaning in the middle of nowhere, where no one could find nor see them. But now, she seemed to have vanished once again.

Could she have been the one who injured Erich Elstrom? Did they have a lover's spat that ended badly? And how could that little lady have gotten the upper hand on such a strong and vigorous man? Unless she had knocked him out by surprise.

"What the hell?" grumbled Vincent Delahousse as he walked around the bed where Sara Lesueur's partner was lying, unconscious, though still alive as they could hear him breathing.

"Maybe some SM games that didn't end well?" one of the policemen suggested. "All tied up like that, it couldn't have been hard for her to knock him out."

Delahousse had seen photos of Sara Lesueur, always dressed to the nines, wearing classical preppy clothing and it was hard for him to imagine her as being a fan of SM games. But external appearances could often be misleading, and the policeman had seen many quirky things and people during his career.

The policemen untied Elstrom and took the scarf off his mouth. Luckily for him, the person who'd tied him up hadn't covered his nose, allowing him to breathe while unconscious. They didn't seem to want to kill him, just to prevent him from moving, reduce him to helplessness. To allow the young lady to flee.

To escape from Elstrom's influence and hold?

To go back home to her family?

And if she had gotten away, where was she now?

And why hadn't she simply taken Erich's car, as they'd found his car keys in his pocket?

"We have to contact the gendarmerie around here and get a search set up," Delahousse ordered.

"That's gonna be fun with this weather and in these mountains," one of his men grumbled.

"Hey Max, if you thought it was going to be a pleasure cruise, you should have done something else. In the meanwhile, get that search job set up. There's a young lady, maybe she's injured" — he was referring to the traces of blood on the floor in the first room — "in the fucking middle of nowhere, each minute could count for her survival. Get going!"

Which he did. While they were speaking, Erich Elstrom, who they'd put a sheet over to mask his intimacy, began to stir on the mattress, slowly emerging from his unconsciousness.

"And find us a doctor!" shouted Delahousse to Max.

Elstrom groaned, stretched, tried to say a few words though they were intelligible to the cops.

"Mr. Elstrom?" asked Delahousse, sitting down on the bed. "Can you hear me? How do you feel?"

"*Mmmmmmm...*"

"And?"

"*Saraaa...*"

That's right, Sara. Sara Lesueur?"

His eyes were now wide open. He winced and raised his hand to his temple, touched the dried blood and frowned once again when he passed his hand over the hematomas and bump on his forehead.

"Yes," he confirmed.

"Was she here with you?"

He nodded.

"Did you kidnap her?"

"No."

"You are lovers?"

A new nod.

"Did she run away?"

Erich closed his eyes to try to recollect, but as he was still half out of it, he gave up.

"I... don't... know. I don't feel good."

"We called a doctor, don't worry. Go and get dressed, I'll be next door."

Delahousse left the room, closed the door behind him and waited, looking around the room, just like a hunting dog trying to sniff out a clue.

Outside of the drops of blood on the floor, Sara's cell phone, or at least what was left of it and her jacket, there was nothing that could shed any light on what could have happened in the past few hours. If of course, you disregarded that huge dildo, the riding crop and the Nazi uniform they'd found in the bedroom.

Those two must have had a jolly good time in their den with all those accessories. Of course, Elstrom must have been wearing the uniform, Sara would have drowned in it. Delahousse was imagining those two playing role games. Both of them. One of them dominant, the other submissive. That was nothing new under the sun, he'd known many an illegitimate couple who satisfied their fancies and desires outside of their homes. They nonetheless usually just rented a hotel room not too far from their workplace and didn't bother driving two hours away from where they lived, in the middle of nowhere, to a god-forsaken cabin in the mountains.

That place continued to intrigue him.

"Mr. Elstrom, do you own this chalet?" he asked when he had finished getting dressed and he'd slowly made his way into the living room about fifteen minutes later.

The man plopped himself down in the chair facing the policeman, his head bowed.

"Yes, I do."

"Are you feeling any better? Can I ask you a few questions?"

Elstrom agreed.

"Can you tell me what you remember about your little stay here with Mrs. Lesueur?"

The man sighed and bit his lip before answering.

"Sara and I had hooked up about eight months ago. She'd decided to leave her husband for me. Like we did each time, we met in the Mucem's parking lot in Marseille. But this time was supposed to be the last time. We'd decided to come here, where no one knew us, to think about our future. We were prepared to leave the south of France."

"You didn't force her then?"

"Of course not! She'd consented to… everything!"

"So what happened here then?"

"Adult games. I'm sure you don't want to know any details."

Delahousse certainly didn't.

"Why did Sara leave? When? And why is her jacket

still here? Why didn't she take your car when she thought of taking her purse?"

"I have no idea," stammered the man, still a bit out of it. "Maybe she decided to walk."

"Sort of dangerous, in my opinion. You don't remember when she left? Was she the one who tied you to the bed? You couldn't have done it yourself, you're not Houdini!"

"I can't remember. I remember her asking me to tie her up, because she liked being dominated and at my mercy. We did our little... *things*, and then I untied her. After that we had an argument."

"Ah? What about?" asked Delahousse.

"She suddenly realized what her decision entailed and panicked. For the future. She was afraid of leaving everything and starting over. Of having made a poor choice, you know stuff like that. She wanted to leave and go back home to her family."

"And you didn't want her to? You made her understand your point of view?"

"After that argument, I can't remember a thing, I'm sorry."

"It'll come back to you," the policeman hoped. Right then his colleague walked in with a doctor from Estoublon, the closest town to the chalet.

The doctor escorted Erich Elstrom into the bedroom to examine him and the policeman picked up his phone. It didn't matter what time it was — two thirty in the morning — he knew that the person he was calling would answer.

CHAPTER 42
Engorged with Blood

Summer 2008

THE SUMMER *of 2008 was a turning point in his life.*

But not in the way he would have liked. He'd imagined a dream vacation, he'd ardently hoped that this would be the year he'd become a man, a real one, that he would no longer have to pretend.

For him, becoming a man meant that he'd no longer have to satisfy himself alone, in his bed with his daydreams. It meant receiving kisses and hugs. It meant having his little stiff thingy enter into that immense mysterious place that the girls have between their legs, that nearly unreachable yet so sought-after chasm. It meant doing the same things he saw on his DVD porn, but better, without this or with more of that, because he still was able to differentiate movies and reality. And the biggest difference was that in the movies, everything seemed so simple.

What he wanted was to really do it, in real life! Even if it was only once. Even if it wouldn't last. He knew it only too well, he could feel it, that "first time" that everyone talked about at that age was merely a sad and failed trial, too short, as much too desired. In and out, wham bam, thank you ma'am, though still full of adolescent frustrations. Maybe ten comings and goings at the very most, like when he'd put the palm of his hand around his penis and rub it up and down just a few seconds before wiping is tacky fingers off.

He knew all of that, so many guys even boasted about it in front of him, trying to play those with experience, those already tired of it. Yeah, sure! Isn't there a saying that goes that the one who talks about it the most is the one who does it the least?

That was why he never talked about it. Though he couldn't get it out of his head.

And that summer, it was the only thing he could think about. His whole body ached, he was thinking about it so hard: his head, his gut, between his legs, and his heart too a bit.

But he couldn't do it, he didn't know how. Plus, he was sure that he was ugly; he looked at his pimply pockmarked face in the bathroom mirror each morning.

So he lost hope, he hoped, he lost himself.

Up till that day in July of 2008. Today. Unless being like that was just losing yourself a tad deeper in his adolescent psychosis.

. . .

The basketball game had just ended, and he and his teammates had lost. Once again. No big deal though, he was an expert in loser's philosophy. Better at that than shooting three-point balls or free throws.

After the game, pain and sweat, it was time to take a shower, what he feared the most. For him changing rooms were a synonym for torture. You have to strip yourself of your jersey, shorts and underwear and run off quickly to the shower. The problem though in those changing rooms was that they were designed ages ago, by some incompetent, negligent or vicious architect who hadn't seen fit to imagine individual shower cabins. Unless he didn't have the budget for that. It was a square room, tiled up to the ceiling, with a dozen showerheads hooked onto three and a half walls, of course the last half was to enter, obviously without a door. Budget, budget!

At first he'd refused to go in with his teammates, who couldn't have cared less about their nudity. At his age when your body is transforming it isn't easy to feel at ease, it's hard to embrace your body's changes, to affirm yourself amongst others. Even though everyone touted the frank camaraderie athletes had, when you find yourself washing your dick next to the members of your team and they compare their attributes to yours, this is a moment that could be traumatic.

Little by little though, you get used to it. He quickly dashed under the shower, washed and rinsed himself, turning his back to his colleagues, right up against the wall, preferring that they see his backside rather than his front. Up till then, no big deal.

Up till that day in the summer of 2008 when everything was overturned.

Once again he was there, shampooing his hair below the tepid shower in the changing rooms of the school where they'd played that afternoon. There were ten of them, the five key players and the ones on the bench, all taking showers between those four walls. Why was that day different from the others? Why did he feel they were spying on him more than usual? Why did the look his neighbor on the right gave him weigh on him more than the other times?

Out of the corner of his eye, he noticed that the other guy was observing him taking his shower, really looking at him. He could distinguish the wry smile he had on his lips while eyeing him from head to toe. He could feel him taking his time looking at his neck, his butt, his sex. A gourmet and appreciative look.

But one that strangely didn't bother him that time. He nearly felt flattered: that was the first time he'd sparked an ounce of interest or attraction from anyone. Of course, he'd always dreamed about the opposite sex. But paradoxically one of his grandpa's sayings ran through his head.

Half a loaf is better than none.

Why not? He was troubled. His neighbor in the shower was good-looking. A well-toned body, nice butt, huge pecs, well-shaped biceps, flat abs, sort of like a chocolate bar that he surprised himself wanting to take a bite out of... What was happening to him? Suddenly his eyes dropped to his neighbor's suds-covered sex. A nice wide and long one, that his neighbor was carefully and slowly washing while looking at him from the corner of his eye, as if trying to make sure he was paying attention.

That attraction both delighted him and made him uncomfortable. He now was upset, embarrassed, torn between desire and shame. Perhaps it was less impressive to be nude amongst other guys rather than with a girl who was getting undressed in front of him? Why not take the easy way out?

Around them there was a loud background noise made from laughter, whistling, swearing about the defeat, that both surrounded and isolated them just as much as the water vapor in the showers. The other guy continued his little hand game, his penis was getting larger. He didn't seem embarrassed at all by that situation.

He quickly finished rinsing himself, got out of the showers and put a towel around his waist before going back into the changing rooms.

A few instants later, the other guy, completely nude and at ease, joined him. They knew each other, were colleagues without being friends. He sat down on the bench next to him.

"We sure got beat bad there."

"We sure did. They were better than us, but we knew that before we came."

"We'll do better next time."

"We will, it can't be any worse."

While talking, they both got dressed, he was squirming trying to get his briefs on under his towel, the other was standing, totally at ease. He looked at him.

"How about training at my place? My parents are gone this weekend, they went to see my grandparents, but I stayed home because of the match. I've got the whole house to myself for two whole days!"

"I'll have to ask my parents."

"Hey! You're sixteen! Come on, it's vacation, you should be having fun. We've got a basketball hoop in the driveway, we can train shooting baskets. After that, have a nice evening. I can order a couple of pizzas for us, we'll listen to my CDs, how about that? A friend's night out."

"Sounds good. I'll ask and see what they say."

That very same evening, his fate slipped down a slope he hadn't suspected until then.

After having played basketball for two hours they were exhausted and both plopped down on the sofa with three pizzas and a pack of 1664, listening to music on the TV.

They ate, drank, and got to know each other better.

Psychologically.

Physically.

It began with a little nothing, without thinking about it.

A gesture, a trembling hand that ventured onto his jeans, that undid a belt, that unzipped a zipper, that slipped in through its opening, that put its fingers around a still flaccid sex, but one that quickly became engorged with blood, appreciative of the caresses.

Without thinking things over, the hand continued like that. Instinctively.

Or out of frustration. A bet.

An experience, a repressed feeling let loose.

That's how it all started.

How would it finish?

He was far from suspecting the consequences of that evening in the summer of 2008.

CHAPTER 43
Lethargy

HOW COULD we have slept when the destiny of my sister was being played out, someplace that night, someplace away from her home?

Jerome, Damien and I were vegetating in the living room, in the middle of bottles of alcohol that were open or empty, waiting to hear some news, whatever it was, about Sara.

About two thirty in the morning, when I finally dozed off with my head on Jerome's lap, I suddenly was woken up. Damien had jumped up like a robot to answer his phone.

As his features changed during the conversation and with the few words he pronounced, I understood that he was talking to Captain Delahousse. I also understood, and that's what shook me out of my lethargy, that the news wasn't the best.

He hung up and looked at us sadly.

"They found out where Sara was, but she was gone. Fuck!"

I closed my eyes and squeezed my eyelids hard to prevent myself from crying, I'd already cried a river. I pushed my lips tightly together so I wouldn't scream and wake Justine up in the middle of the night. Jerome was also despondent.

"What did he say to you?" he asked.

Our brother-in-law summed up what the policeman had told him. The chalet between the mountains, ravines, and forests. The discovery of Sara's broken cell phone. The confirmation of her adulterous relationship with someone named Erich Elstrom, who was safe and sound, attached to a bed, whereas Sara was missing. Her purse that wasn't there, her jacket that was. And no leads to indicate where she could be, at this time of the night. And her lover's car that was still there, with the keys in it. Plus the search that the local cops organized to try to find my sister in the midst of that dense forest in the pouring rain.

When all was said and done, we were basically in the same place as a few hours ago. For days, it had been like a roller coaster, with thin hopes and vast disillusions. That made me think of the expression: *jumping from the frying pan into the fire*. Just like that person, things were getting worse and worse for us, pushing both of us down into deep and bottomless abysses.

After a long silence populated with interrogations, pain and embarrassments, I reached another conclusion that seemed to hold water for me.

"What if we've been wrong since the beginning?"

"What do you mean?" asked Jerome, intrigued.

"In the way we interpreted the messages that our anonymous harasser sent. What if we got ahead of ourselves by associating Sara's first name with the Sara mentioned in the Bible? And if, instead of bringing us closer to the solution, they'd tried to distance us from the true target on purpose? Which brings us back to our initial problem: who is that potential victim? Who else is really endangered, who else could be killed, right now, here in France or elsewhere?"

That question paralyzed us for a moment.

"Sara's not the target then?" asked Damien, astonished.

"And why not ? That's what I'm wondering right now. Wondering if our case and the one concerning you and Sara, if they're not related to each other at all. I mean, and excuse me for what I'm gonna say now, but I've got like the impression that my sister just ran off with her lover…"

Damien was shaking his head while listening to me, not at all convinced.

"She wouldn't have vanished into thin air like that, leaving him attached to a bed after having knocked him out. Plus she ran off on foot, in the forest, in the middle of the night, in pouring rain. And to go where? Come back here? That's impossible. I mean it's a two-hour drive!"

I sighed.

"I know, that seems crazy, but not impossible. Maybe she'll give us some news, some way or another."

"If we don't find her dead at the bottom of some ravine," concluded Damien in a grim voice.

CHAPTER 44
Filth

FOR THE ENTIRE NIGHT, with pounding rain that made the ground slippery and muddy, the policemen searched the area for any eventual traces that could lead to locating Sara Lesueur. They looked around everything close to the chalet, searching through ravines, fields, rivers, forests, ditches next to the roads, but to no avail. Then they extended their research towards the neighboring hamlets, then the nearest villages and towns.

In the morning, they tried to question any eventual witnesses, but no one seemed to care about what could have happened near them during the preceding night and day.

Yet, when the sun finally came up, one of the investigators who was examining the ground next to the chalet, found a mysterious element. He kneeled to see it better, looked down, put his fingers on the ground and got up again. He walked a few feet to reach Erich Elstrom's vehicle, — who had been taken to the hospital and asked to remain at the police force's disposition as a witness — and the four-wheel drive of the police from Marseille, kneeled again to inspect both of their tires and walked back to where he had been before.

"Cap, come here a second."

Delahousse, with a haggard face as he'd been up all night, slowly walked over.

"Yeah, Julien? You find something? You look like a truffle dog who's found a buried mushroom."

"Look at those tire tracks. I don't think they match those of the other two vehicles."

"I think you're right," Delahousse admitted, after having checked the same thing his subordinate had. "But it's hard to conclude anything, when you think of all the cars around here last night."

He was talking about several gendarmerie vehicles as well as the doctor's car.

The policeman had to admit that his boss wasn't wrong but stuck to his guns. Deep down inside something was tickling him. He snapped a few photos of the tire tracks and walked off.

The investigators gathered all the evidence that they had about this investigation, putting the pieces of Sara's cell phone, the Nazi officer uniform, the young lady's jacket and a few other miscellaneous objects into plastic bags and then into a cardboard box that they put in the trunk.

They were hesitating about whether to drive back to Marseille now but decided to rent some rooms in the closest hotel to rest. One of them drove Erich Elstrom's car to the hospital parking lot, where he had been admitted.

When he got back to the police station the next afternoon, Captain Delahousse decided to look over all the evidence of what they'd taken from the chalet.

That was when, while examining Sara Lesueur's jacket, he discovered a piece of paper in one of the pockets that left him completely flummoxed, and understandably so.

He thought he'd shed light on a good portion of the recent events implicating the Bastaro couple and the Lesueur family, but that was an unexpected turn of events. The unpredictable and intellectually stimulating aspects he ran across in his police investigations were one of the reasons why he'd chosen this line of work.

Such unexpected developments didn't happen every day, that was life, usually ghastly trivial, but a surprise like that had the gift of restoring his faith in his job.

When he read that little piece of paper he'd found in an inner pocket in Sara's jacket, his eyes opened with astonishment. As big as a Post-it, it was covered with a tiny and elegant handwriting, undoubtedly feminine.

The few words on it baffled him even more.

. . .

COLOMBE, my sweet little sister, I'm so sorry. You think you know your family, but sometimes you don't. Below the varnish on the mask, you often find filth. I have to take this idea to its logical conclusion. Sara.

CHAPTER 45

Asking for forgiveness

THE NEXT DAY all three of us were asked to come to the police station at the end of the afternoon.

Jerome, Damien and I had only slept for a couple of hours, hardly restorative sleep, before Justine woke us up again. Her dad drove her to school as he thought she'd be better off there rather than staying at home with us and our unhappiness. He told her that it would be her friend Anais's mom who'd pick her up and then she'd go to their house for an after-school snack and a play date. The little girl accepted without saying a word.

So we all went to meet up with Captain Delahousse, in the second district police station, where he'd set up a temporary office.

What an uncomfortable situation that was for my husband, my brother-in-law and me to be between the four walls of that police station, in response to the summons of an investigator who hadn't wanted to speak with us on the phone about what he'd recently discovered. Was it that bad or crucial that he had to tell us face to face?

We went into his office expecting the worst.

"Sit down, please. How are you?"

We all said we were completely distraught and devastated by the stressful days we'd had. You could tell just by looking at us.

"Is it that bad?" Damien couldn't help but ask.

Delahousse sat down, putting his hands together in front of his mouth as he usually did when saying delicate things.

"Bad, I don't know yet. Original and unsettling, that I do know."

"Please tell us," I implored him.

Instead of answering me, the captain handed me a piece of paper.

"Here, it's for you."

"For me?" I stammered.

"Yes, you personally. I discovered it in your sister's jacket that she forgot — probably on purpose — in the chalet."

I read Sara's words.

Almost choking with incomprehension.

And broke down in tears.

I'd never cried so much in my life as I had recently, since we got married a week ago. Ironic, isn't it.

Then I handed the message to Jerome, he read it and gave it to Damien. That way we all had the same info.

That new element challenged all of our previous reasoning and deductions. Everything we'd imagined up till then fell over like a fragile house of cards.

The most difficult thing was to correctly assess that new situation, what it meant, and I tried to sum it up in a few words.

"I'm afraid to understand this... I can't believe that Sara was the one..."

"Who was at the origin of the messages?" Jerome completed my sentence.

"No, I can't believe that," I insisted. "Yet, if you read this well, she seems to be apologizing for what she did, for what she seems to be wanting to do..."

"That can't be Sara," Damien objected.

He picked up that note once again.

"But it is her handwriting, there's no doubt about that."

"I confirm. But where is she? Captain, you didn't find any trace of her?"

"No, she literally seems to have vanished into thin air. We have no idea where, nor how nor why exactly. Except for the confession and apology addressed to you. What bothers me in this story is that we were sure that the author of those threats could only have been a man."

"That's probably what they wanted us to believe to lead us on a wild goose chase, once again," I added. "Ever since the beginning, the threats talk about a game that the author likes playing. And here, isn't she talking about a mask?"

"She's also insinuating that you never really know those people you're close to," Jerome added, looking at me.

"After what just happened, I have to admit that I'm no longer sure that I even know my own sister," I was forced to admit.

Right then thoughts ran helter-skelter through my mind. I recalled our wedding, where Sara had hugged me, kissed me, and had been so happy for us. Also the chamber pot ritual that she took part in, where I could tell she was sincere and having fun. Then I thought back on when we were teens, on our complicity back then. We were inseparable, in total osmosis, almost like twin sisters. How could I imagine that Sara, the Sara of my souvenirs, wanted to destroy our lives? No, that was completely out of the question.

"Mrs. Bastaro, I understand your distress," Delahousse said, trying to reassure me. "Still though, even if that doesn't lead to anything, I think we're going to have to go back to square one here. Start with the letter that you found in your wedding urn. Then reread each message received since then, reinterpreting them from a different point of view. As of right now, we don't have anything more concrete than that."

Which was what we then did with the captain, rereading the first message, then the various anonymous emails, and finally that typed letter we found in our mailbox at home.

But our four brains working together in the police station didn't find anything else that day. We had to face the facts: we were back where we'd begun. The only constant that seemed interesting to us resided in our conviction that our torturer was someone we knew, someone close to us who knew about our life and our past. It also seemed clear to us that this person knew where we were, what we were doing, and could also anticipate our movements and even our thoughts.

That was terrifying.

After two hours the captain let us exit the police station, though he asked us to keep on thinking.

"Maybe when you least expect it, something will seem evident to you," he hoped.

He also told us when we were leaving that the police would continue their investigations to try to find who was the author of those anonymous messages.

When we arrived at my sister's house in Rousset, her absence made us even sadder, and that day drew to an end in complete despondence.

All we could do was wait... for a fatal outcome?

CHAPTER 46
Youth is a shipwreck

COMBING his hair with his hands instead of a comb in his abundant salt-and-pepper colored hair, the man hunkered down in his armchair, holding a glass of cold beer. The end of another tough day. It had begun very early that morning and would continue in two or so hours, after a quick dinner. That was why he allowed himself to have a well-deserved beer during his break.

Of course, he couldn't drink a lot in his line of work. Driving while inebriated wasn't generally appreciated by those in charge. Just a bit over the limit and you'd have to pay a huge fine plus you'd lose points on your driver's license.

So no, he was going to be careful, especially now. That would be really too bad.

He took a long slug from his glass followed by a hefty and liberating burp that smelled like hops. No one would bother him for burping at home, and he wouldn't lose any points on his politeness license, not that it actually existed.

He was so satisfied with his wit that he began to chuckle while another belch escaped him.

"Jesus Christ does that ever feel great!" he said out loud before finishing his beer.

He glanced at a box he'd brought down from the attic the day before. He had been quite nostalgic lately and wanted to revisit his souvenirs as a teen. That was when he'd remembered that box he'd stored up in the attic years ago and forgotten about. He was hoping it contained photos of him and his friends when they were younger, their *golden years*, as some people called them. That was right, their golden innocence, their awareness of life, their transition to adulthood: adolescence! That was what people said, but most of them had forgotten everything. His memory was good though.

You had to work to remember things. You had to relive your memories regularly. That was what he was doing when he put his glass of beer down on the coffee table and opened the box full of yellowish photos.

He grabbed a handful of them. They were in different sizes, of varying quality. Some were completely botched, others were magnificent. Sometimes funny, sometimes sad or even moving.

Generally speaking, all those hormone-filled teen faces gave him a rosy picture. For one or two who were good-looking, there was a myriad of unattractive, disgraceful and pimply faced others. And those horrible haircuts! And ugly sweaters! And Coke-bottle glasses! And those smiles showing off braces! *Youth is a shipwreck*, he thought, playing with words de Gaulle had pronounced about General Petain. He was a man without a lot of culture, but that was a quote he'd always liked.

Glancing at a hundred or so photos, abandoned without any order in the box, he suddenly stopped when he saw one of them, one that sent him back twenty years. He perhaps was unconsciously looking for that one? Whatever, but that photo didn't leave him indifferent, far from it! It rekindled forgotten feelings in his unfulfilled desires, and poorly digested regrets.

It was summer, he was sure of that, you just had to look at the swimsuits.

Of course it was hot, everyone was sweating.

Love was in the air, he could tell by their vague looks.

OF COURSE he recognized himself immediately. How could he not have? He was so... remarkable! So... different! So... unique!

He quickly identified the others too. He had a good facial memory (and hadn't forgotten the sexy curves either.) He was better at remembering faces than names. The same thing was true at work, he never forgot a client and could recall them even years later. And as God was his witness, he had a slew of clients!

Anyway, that photo stirred him enormously because of the nostalgia emanating from it, sparked by the events of the last few days. Like the poet Eluard said: *There is no such thing as a chance encounter.* Something he easily believed right now.

He'd made an appointment with the past, which had met the present, in his memory and in his actions.

HE SUDDENLY HEARD some muffled moaning and whimpering downstairs which woke him from his daydreaming. And luckily so, because when he glanced at the clock on the wall, he realized that he had to get going or he'd be late.

He threw the photo on the table with the others, next to his empty glass with a bit of foam on top and put a jacket on. Before leaving he quickly prepared a bowl of water and another one of food and opened the basement door.

The pallid light in the basement flicked on and off while he was going downstairs. The moans increased in intensity, a shape was stirring in one of the corners. He carefully approached it.

"You gonna zip it?" he said putting the bowls down on the floor.

The whines turned into muffled noises mixed with a squeaking sound.

"I have to leave now. You just calm down. I don't want the neighbors to hear you and complain, so shut the hell up!"

The man raised his hand in a threatening gesture, one that ordered respect and obedience.

The shape curled up in the corner, docile, cajoling.

"There you go! That's better. You're beginning to understand."

The gray-haired man went upstairs, turned the light off, making it quite dark in the basement that was merely dimly lit up by a bottom hung opening in which natural lighting of the setting sun penetrated with difficulty.

He slammed the door shut and locked it, putting the key in his jacket.

He left, locked the front door and got into his taxi.

He turned the key, activated the meter attached to his rear-view mirror, clicked the "empty" mode which lit the light attached to the roof of the car and put it in drive.

He liked working at night.

CHAPTER 47
Intellectual masturbation

DAMIEN, Jerome and I had now spent two whole days without any news from Sara. Captain Delahousse's investigation was also treading water.

Once again he'd interviewed Erich Elstrom as a witness, but all he could do was to give him the gritty details of his liaison with my sister. An adulterous relationship based on deviant though consensual sexual games. They were like a couple of sex friends, a trendy notion nowadays if you could believe the smutty people magazines that published that type of juicy gossip. To sum it up, neither Sara nor he hurt anyone except the family members who now knew about it. They were responsible consenting adults, nothing reprehensible about that.

Except...

Except that their story didn't end well, slipping off at a given time to sink into an unthinkable and terrible apprehension.

The apprehension we were drowning in right now.

As there was nothing new, we'd decided to stay in Rousset with Damien. We wouldn't be more productive at home in Biscarrosse, so we might as well stick together and think things over — again and again! —, in hopes of reaching some hypothetical explanation about Sara's disappearance.

We unrelentingly pooled our efforts and brainstormed to try to decipher the elements we had in our possession, which didn't amount to much actually. Only what that wacko wanted us to have. He — or she? — was the one setting the pace and all we could do was try to follow.

But though we did rack our brains, nothing came out of that sterile intellectual masturbation. All we could do now is wait until the next step, the one *they* were leading us to.

Both of us were in a terrible state. Our exhaustion and lack of sleep without counting our permanent stress was turning us into limp, nearly catatonic puppets.

My little niece, that adorable little Justine, was starting to think it was strange that Mommy had been gone for so long and she also risked a depression, something four-year-old kids certainly shouldn't have to endure. Luckily for us, she still had school and played with her best friend for a few hours after each day, as her parents were both understanding and caring.

Damien had taken a few days off; it would have been

impossible for him to work in his state. As for us, as we were both freelancers, we had a lot of freedom. What was the most ironic was that after our wedding, we'd decided to take two weeks off for rest and relaxation. You could say that our goals of *rest* and *relaxation* hadn't been met!

Jerome had begun to think out loud and blurted out an idea that didn't seem bad to me.

"And what about letting your cousin Bertrand in on all this? I know you don't want to let your whole family know about this, but doesn't he work in IT? I think he vaguely mentioned that to me last week when we were having cocktails."

"He does, he's a programmer for some subsidiary of Arianespace in Toulouse, something like that, one of those things I don't understand anything about."

"In that case, maybe he'd be able to help us find out who sent those anonymous messages?"

"Like he'd be better than the police cyber-investigators?"

"You never know. *Nothing ventured, nothing gained*, like the old saying goes. We could always ask. If he can, he can, if he can't, well it's no big deal. At least we'll have tried something rather than going around in circles like a lion in a cage with the same questions and lack of answers."

I actually thought that was a good idea my dear hubby had. We thought that at this point it was too bad if we threw a bit of ballast overboard to a few family members, as long as those vulnerable ones like our parents or grandparents had no idea of what was happening.

I looked up my cousin's name in my contacts and clicked on it.

It went through to his voicemail.

"Hi, Bertrand, this is Colombe. I hope you're doing well. As for us, it's a little complicated. I'd like to ask you for a service, it's urgent. Can you call me back ASAP? Thanks, talk soon."

In the meanwhile, to try to relax, Jerome and I decided to go jogging in the magnificent scenery around Rousset, dominated by Mont Sainte Victoire. Jogging through vineyards and olive gardens, we aired out our lungs and tried to heal our broken souls. We tried to exhale all of that darkness that had accumulated in our hearts for the past ten days.

I'd taken my phone and placed it in my chest harness where I also had put my water bottle. When it rang, I sat down on a flat rock to answer it, looking at the majestic Mount Sainte Victoire, whose name made me hope we'd also soon have a victory.

"Hey! Colombine, it's cousin Bert! What's all this rush about?"

In the next half an hour, while Jerome was stretching, leaning on a pole in the vineyard, I told my cousin in Toulouse the whole story, starting off with the letter we'd found in the urn up until Sara's incredible disappearance.

"Jesus Christ!" was all he could say.

I understood. Hard to swallow a story like that, especially summed up in such a short time.

"Yup. That's why we thought maybe you could help us here Bertrand. You're like our last hope."

"I'm not Superman either. I don't have any magical powers."

"I know, but you're really good in IT, the web and all that stuff."

"Yeah, that's true, I do have a few skills in that field. You never know till you try. Of course I'll help you. What did you think? That I'd just close the door on you? To tell you the truth I'm going to make that my number one priority."

A sigh just as long as my arm escaped from my mouth, with this glimmer of hope.

"Thanks in advance Bertrand. From the bottom of my heart. I didn't want you to get mixed up in this, but I don't have a choice here. I hope you're not angry with me."

"Are you kidding Colombe? That's what families are all about, standing side by side. So here's what we're gonna do. You're going to start by sending me everything you told me about. Those emails, messages, everything! Plus Sara's phone number, I don't think I have it, and Damien's too. And also that Elstrom guy's phone, if the cops say you can. Send all that to me on my email, Bertrand.Signol@gmail.com. Ah! One more thing. The list of all the guests at your wedding with their contact details, the one you gave to the cops. Plus you'll have to allow me to install some software on your phone, to try to find out where those messages you got came from. I'm not going to bore you with all the technical terms now, but believe me, I'm not going to ogle any of your sexy photos with Jerome, or any other newlywed stuff."

My cousin burst out laughing, happy he'd made me laugh. And it did me a world of good too, to hear him chuckling! I'd begun to believe that it was something that no longer existed!

"Thanks so much Bertrand, I'll send you everything right now."

I had a miniscule glimmer of hope, but it was certainly better than nothing.

CHAPTER 48
Heil Hitler!

A TINY BEAM of light made it through below the still closed door. The shadows of the night were disappearing through the tiny window in the room, slowly lighting up the young lady curled up at an angle of the room with its wooden walls.

Her ankles were throbbing from the chains that held her attached to some pipework on the wall. This time it was no longer an adult game.

It seemed like it was ages ago, an instant of oblivion and abandon she'd shared with her lover, Erich, in that isolated little cottage in the middle of Verdon Park. Things were starting to come back to her now.

She remembered their last moments together, when they'd had that argument after she'd informed him she wanted to go back to Marseille, back to her family, back to her daughter, because she was no longer sure she'd made the right decision by fleeing them.

She didn't have enough time to realize what was

happening to her. Everything went so quickly. Erich had tossed her cell phone into the air, and it made a huge curve before shattering itself against one of the walls and falling to the floor. Then her lover had caught up with her as she was trying to leave and had carried her back into the bedroom.

She was reliving that scene, which happened very quickly, as if she were watching a slomo scene at the movies.

She remembered having fleetingly seen the door of the chalet opening, in Erich's back, despite the huge stature of her lover that partially blocked her view.

Then she saw a silhouette enter the room. Even in slowmo, she was unable to associate a face with the shadow that had swooped down on them. Also because the person who'd just come in was wearing a mask.

Undoubtedly a man though, because of his corpulence.

Still in slowmo in her mind, Sara visualized the object the man was holding, a colored baseball bat. Then she saw him swing it around and violently hit Erich's skull. Her lover then released his grip like a spring and the young lady fell while Erich lurched around like a drunkard. Then he collapsed like a disarticulated puppet whose strings holding it up had been cut and passed out.

That masked man then dominated Sara. She wanted to scream, but was paralyzed by fear, with her mouth open, just like a carp someone had fished out of a river, lacking oxygen.

The unknown man put a finger in front of his lips, in the universal gesture to be quiet.

"*Shhh*! You're gonna be a good girl, aren't you?"

Sara wanted to flee, but the man grabbed her wrist, rekindling her pain.

"I said good girl! Or do you want me to tie you up?" he threatened.

She shook her head "no," several times quickly, now terrorized.

"Help me then. Grab him by the feet," he ordered designating Erich with a movement of his chin.

Which she did.

They dragged the unconscious body to the bedroom.

"Now let's strip this pig."

She helped him undress Erich, now lying on the bed. The unknown man took his boxers off and grabbed Elstrom's flaccid penis and pulled it, as if he wanted to pull it off, before finally letting go with a contemptuous growl.

"You're cheating on your husband for this limp dick?"

Sara wondered how that person could know so many things about her and her lover.

After that they tied Erich to the bed using the scarves and handcuffs that Sara had used earlier. The man visibly liked staging things. Then he sniggered when he saw the Nazi uniform.

"Heil Hitler!" he said, raising an arm.

Sara's legs had given out and she collapsed against the wall of the bedroom, her arms crossed on her legs.

"Come on! Time to go! You coming or not?"

Sara, paralyzed by fear, couldn't even budge. The authoritarian man walked up to her, grabbed an elbow and brutally stood her up.

"Fuck! I didn't want it to be like this. You're not making things easy for me. Tough shit, I'm going to have to be more persuasive."

"What do you want with me?" Sara stammered.

"I don't really know yet, I have to think things over. So in the meanwhile, just come."

She tried to fight him off, which sparked a powerful reaction. His fist connected with her forehead, and she collapsed, unconscious.

Now attached to the pipework, that was the last thing that Sara remembered in the Verdon Park chalet.

She had no idea what had happened next.

She didn't feel him injecting something into her arm.

When the man took her in his arms to carry her to the back seat of the car, she was unconscious.

She didn't see the miles go by that night in the Alps-de-Haute-Provence region nor when they crossed through other counties.

She didn't see them arrive either, incapable of estimating how many hours they'd been on the road.

She had no idea where she was.

She only woke up once she was there, in that dark room with its wooden walls, attached to a pipe, her ankles aching, her mouth parched and her stomach growling from hunger.

Sara had to stretch as far as she could to reach the bowls he'd given her. One of them was filled with water, the other with some kind of mysterious food she couldn't identify. Whatever, she was thirsty and starving.

She put her arm out, dragged the bowl over closer and used her fingers to eat. The meat had a strong taste, but she couldn't afford to be picky. She winced while swallowing.

Then when she felt full, she brought the water bowl closer and drank a bit of that tepid liquid, without any pleasure, only because of necessity.

What day are we? she wondered.

When had she left her home in Rousset? How long since she'd seen her daughter? An eternity. Her emotional pain was stronger than her physical suffering. She broke down in tears and laid down on the cold floor of that dark room.

Her sobs and convulsions woke her bladder up. She hadn't urinated for hours. Yet it wasn't that tiny bit of water she'd drank that made her want to urinate, it was a mere physiological need; you couldn't keep yourself from peeing for an indefinite amount of time!

She tried to hold it back, but unsuccessfully. She couldn't stand having such a full bladder. She had to relieve herself, at any cost.

She looked at her ankles tied together and sighed. She couldn't just pee sitting there, just like a dog whose hind legs are paralyzed.

She couldn't even take her pants off completely because of her ankles being attached. She did her utmost to lower them as far as possible, as well as her underwear, and then dragged herself as far as she could. Then she squatted.

Her subconscious thoughts paradoxically prevented her from letting go and she had to force herself. Finally the warm liquid evacuated itself in a powerful jet, soiling the floor and splashing on her ankles, thighs, as well as a part of her clothing rolled around her calves.

Shame mixed itself with the smell of ammonia in her urine.

Exhausted, she hobbled back to her corner and fell asleep.

CHAPTER 49
Their tired brains

THAT MESSAGE we had both been waiting for and fearing finally arrived.

We didn't care, all we wanted was some news about Sara. Good or bad, whatever it was, the worst part was remaining in total ignorance.

This time it was Damien who got that anonymous email, rather than Jerome or me. At least we appreciated the originality of that process though we certainly didn't appreciate its heinous content.

From: Anonymousemail

Hi there, Damien!
So? How ya doing? Oops, excuse me, I forgot how sad you must be, not having any news about your dear and tender... cheating wife!

Oh! Such language! I'm not one to rub salt into your wounds... No, I'm not a nasty person like that, I just like to joke around. I know, little things have amused me lately. Undoubtedly leftovers of juvenile carelessness. Or maybe I'm still a child who never grew up.

Speaking of which, how is charming little Justine? I hope she's not too sad because her mommy disappeared so suddenly. Young children are so very fragile... You never realize the impact of acts like this on kids of that age. Traces that they could have for their whole lives, permanent ones in some cases! But I'm sure you're doing everything you can to protect her from all of this. You are a very protective person. Just like Auntie Colombe and Uncle Jerome, don't you agree? Because I would presume that they've joined you so that all three of you can support each other in this atrocious and unprecedented ordeal.

Please say hi to them if I'm not asking too much, my dear Damien. I'll let you guess who I am... And I'm actually going to call upon your interpersonal skills, if that's alright with you of course, by naming you as the spokesman to what I want to tell all three of you, to save me from sending them a separate email. Got it? Thanks so much, you are very obliging!

So, I was talking about this atrocious and new ordeal that has been concerning you for the past couple of days. Firstly Colombe and Jerome, then you, after your dear Sara left. Does that make you think that the two cases are linked together? Got me, but why not? Let's explore that hypothesis.

Sara had a roll in the hay with her lover? Who

cares! If that was all it was, it was just a trivial and meaningless adventure. A story of unhappiness or boredom in a couple, a booty call. No big deal.

No, that would be much too easy.

I nonetheless must admit that I did take advantage of her little getaway. Or at least it was quite the windfall in my initial plans.

Anyway, we'll probably have the opportunity to talk about all that later, I can assure you.

And in the meanwhile, let me give you some news about your beloved Sara. Generally speaking, she's fine.

Oh! I can't affirm that she's enjoying all the comfort a woman like her should have, but in the history of humanity, we've seen worse.

For a while I thought about sending you a little video with this note, so she could speak directly with you, but I changed my mind. But maybe because I'm a nice guy, I'll do it next time. Would you like to see her?

Darn it! I just realized that it's materially impossible for you to answer my questions as this is an anonymous email. Maybe next time I'll write with my real name.

Excuse me, I'm having problems writing because I'm laughing so hard.

You have to admit that I've got a great sense of humor!

Let's be serious now though.

Before I leave to go see your dear Sara and take care of her... don't worry, with no ulterior motives, let me reassure you, I'm just going to give Colombe and Jerome a few explanations. I'm hoping that this will ease their tired brains.

You'll tell them Damien, won't you? Thank you. Such a nice guy! I knew I could count on you.

So, this is what you have to tell them. That they should go over my previous messages in the light of this new detail. Meaning that they're all linked together.

I'm sure they haven't forgotten that nice little poem I wrote for them. Don't you think that was a delicate attention? Did they let you read it? Did you appreciate it? I must admit that I'm neither Ronsard nor Baudelaire, but I still know how to make things rhyme.

And I'm sure they haven't forgotten my enigmatic message composed of a list of numbers. Elements which astutely and cunningly led them to Sara.

And if they hadn't seen what they should have?

Please tell them, a tip from me, to reconsider those two messages under the same angle. One linked to the other.

I won't say anything more, I know they're clever enough to shed light on this alone now.

Well, I gotta go now.
See you soon then.
Sincerely yours..."

WE READ the last sentences of that abject message, full of unhealthy irony, completely disgusted. With each sentence we could feel the malicious pleasure he'd had by torturing us with his words and ideas.

The only certainty we now had was that the man who had kidnapped Sara was the one who had threatened us on our wedding day. My sister's disappearance appeared to be one of the pieces of a malefic puzzle that this guy was putting together, for our misfortune.

What was his goal? What was he looking for? And why?

He'd said we'd find out why by examining is previous messages once again, linking them together. So that's what Damien, Jerome and I did after having transferred his latest email to Captain Delahousse.

We reread the poem attentively.

We went through the series of numbers and figures.

We put the two messages side by side on the table.

And a light suddenly came on in my brain, nearly at the same time as in Jerome's.

The truth was staring at us in the face, unsettling, chilling.

CHAPTER 50
Barricaded

MY COUSIN'S phone call was like a double-edged sword. It had brought us an ounce of hope while dampening our enthusiasm.

"Colombe? I think I got something," Bertrand said straightaway.

"Really?"

"I think so. Not something that could tell us where Sara is right away, but what I meant is a new angle of research. I think I understand how to get to the bottom of these messages. That's what I wanted to tell you."

"That's better than nothing. Tell me more."

"The problem is that it's going to take time."

"How much?"

"At this stage, I have no idea. But I'll do everything I can, promise. It's actually quite complex. Want me to explain it to you?"

"If it's not too technical, sure."

"Well it is pretty technical, but I'll try to put it in layman's terms. So, to start with, have you ever heard of the dark web?"

I mentally wrinkled my nose.

"You mean porn? Stuff for pedophiles?"

Bertrand just laughed.

"No, not at all, stuff like that a twelve-year-old can find on the clear web in five minutes."

"The what?"

"The clear web, sites anyone can access! To make it simple, there are three internet levels, three types of websites. In order, you've got the clear web, the deep web, and the dark web."

"Slow down there, you're losing me."

My cousin cleared this throat.

"It's easy to understand. I'll explain using an image. Imagine an iceberg, that's easy. As you know — and as the captain of the Titanic didn't seem to know — the tip of the iceberg only represents about 5 to 10% of its global mass. The remainder, about 95%, is below the water and thus invisible. Where is it immersed? In deep water, like the *deep web*, or even in the dark water of the abysses, like the *dark web*. So, anyone can access the clear web, using any browser, right? You agree?"

"I do."

"Okay. Then then the next submerged layer, the deep web, can also be accessed by anyone. Here I'm talking about sites or pages that are blocked by passwords, like paid content, bank accounts, emails, back offices, etc. Places where you need your passwords to get into. Still following?"

"Up till now."

"Great. Now we'll have a look at the lowest level of that iceberg, the deepest one. That infamous *dark web*. That's where you find sites and pages that can only be accessed using specific networks, specific protocols and configurations. You'll never be able to access those secret applications by traditional browsers. You have to use special routers called TOR, Freenet, I2P, etc."

"You're losing me here."

"Don't worry, I'm not going to delve into any details. To help you understand better, I'll explain what VPN and proxies are... You know, I think your guy barricaded himself behind a completely anonymous network, one that's secret and is protected behind many different layers. What you have to remember is that there are several layers of protection, like an onion, get it? Here, he's sending out messages using the dark web, that's in the heart of the onion, and each layer of it is encrypted by a key. And incidentally the acronym TOR stands for The Onion Router, and all the dark web sites don't finish with *.com*, or *.net* or *.org*, like regular ones but with *.onion*. But that's a mere detail, you can forget it."

"Okay. I'll just remember the onion and the iceberg. So, if I understood correctly, he sent his messages from the protected dark web. Which is why no one can find him."

"You understood the most important stuff."

"That's illegal, isn't it?"

"Not actually. You have to understand that TOR was created by the American Navy, financed by universities, Google, NGOs, etc. It's a way of communicating anonymously, outside of the traditional circuits. For example it's used in countries where the authorities don't always allow freedom of speech and web access, see who I'm talking about?"

"China? North Korea?"

"Others too. Plus whistleblowers also use it, remember the Wikileaks affair and Julian Assange? So, you can't really say that the dark web is intrinsically illegal, but it's true that it often hosts illicit affairs, black market stuff. You can buy drugs, smartphones at discounted prices, weapons, and pay for all that with cryptocurrency, like Bitcoins or Monero. But that's all I'll tell you about the technical aspect. Just all that to explain to you my dear cousin why that will take me a while."

"But it's not impossible?"

"No, *to a valiant heart, nothing is impossible*. I can't promise you anything though. It's really complicated to crack and hack into systems like that."

While Bertrand was talking to me I had an idea.

"What about contacting Captain Delahousse's team? They've got cyber-investigators who work on investigations concerning the web."

"Sure! *Onionted* we stand," my cousin joked. "Sorry, *united*! Give me their contact details and I'll call them. Maybe we'll make faster and more efficient progress together."

"Great. Thanks again, Bertrand. From the bottom of my heart."

"No problem. That's what families are for."

I hung up and told Jerome and Damien about what we'd talked about.

Then we returned to our analysis of the messages — the poem and the numbers — to face that chilling revelation we'd had right before Bertrand called.

CHAPTER 51
An invisible threat

WE HAD BEEN TORTURING our brains trying to read the poem and link it directly to the series of numbers.

We were looking right at it. Certainly not the best poem I'd ever read, but not the worst either. If of course it didn't contain some invisible threat...

The most beautiful thing on earth
  Tell me, it must be
  The love you have for others.
  That powerful feeling
  Can actually sooth
  And become a solution, that
  Is swept away
  By such a lovely impetus.
  Letting your heart speak,

That incredible organ
Where are hidden many closer
Feelings inside...
You must always dare
Tell your loved ones
Much sooner rather than later,
Before you see the Grim Reaper,
That horrible harpy,
Who actually only comes once.
Because though you don't like it,
People may say
They'll escape from its scythe...
When that day comes,
Often by surprise, and
Believe it, that day will come,
For each and every one!

I REMEMBERED that famous letter Georges Sand had written to Alfred de Musset, her lover.

WHEN YOU FIRST READ IT, it is a very beautiful love letter.

She begins by telling him that she realized, the last time they were together, that

he wanted to take her dancing.

Then she adds that she remembers his kiss and saw it as proof that he could love her. She continues and invites him over, saying that she is a sincere and selfless woman, one able to show him both friendship and affection.

She says that living alone is difficult and hard to bear.

George Sand ends this poem by telling him to come over quickly and make

her forget all of this through the love he has for her.
A nice love letter, isn't it?

But, when you read every other line in this poem, and using in a couple of places,

the way some words are cut in two in French, you have a whole different kettle of fish!

Something you wouldn't want your children to read!

Skipping every other line, her poem then goes like this:

I'm very moved to tell you that
I still really want to be fucked,
and I'd like it to be by you.
I'm ready to show you my ass,
and if you want to see me completely nude,
come and pay me a little visit.
I'll prove to you that I'm a sincere and deep woman,
as well as the
narrowest one that you could dream of,
As your dick is very long, hard and often thick,
Run over to see me as quickly as you can and
put it inside me.

. . .

In this letter, you had to read every other line to discover a whole different version, a saucy and naughty one, some would even say pornographic, that only Musset would know about.

I'd tried to do the same with our poem, but in vain. There had to be something else.

The numbers were the key here.

1-1
6-4
7-1
11-3
11-5
15-4
16-2
18-2
20-2
24-1

It suddenly was evident! We had missed a quite simple system. All we had to do was understand that the first number designated the line to be taken into account, meaning the first, sixth, seventh, eleventh, etc. up until the twenty-fourth and last verse.

And the second number corresponded to the word that was important in that verse. Meaning the first one, then the fourth one, then once again the first one.

Those isolated words then formed a simple but meaningful sentence.

1-1: THE
6-4: SOLUTION
7-1: IS
11-3: HIDDEN
11-5: CLOSER
15-4: THAN
16-2: YOU
18-2: MAY
20-2: ACTUALLY
24-1 BELIEVE

"Son of a bitch! *The solution is hidden closer than you may actually believe...*" I repeated. "What is he talking about now?"

I thought I had an idea about the hidden meaning of that affirmation. But first I had to define what he meant by *closer*.

"Close or closer can have several meanings," Jerome began. "You can live *close to here, closer to someone* than someone else, indicating some physical or spatial proximity.

"Or *closer in time*, meaning something that's *imminent*," added Damien.

"But also a *close* friend, a family member."

I shook my head, lost in our attempts to find some meaning about what had happened to us for the past week.

"But does *closer* refer to the victim or the author?

I've sort of got the feeling that this is like a snake biting its tail, we're in a vicious circle. Remember that we got the poem and that list of numbers *before* Sara was kidnapped. Maybe that was what he wanted us to understand: that the solution was *close* because my sister was the victim! So, even if we arrived at that conclusion mistakenly, using those Bible verses, we still were right. The facts unfortunately prove that Sara was the one targeted. And that last email we got confirms this: the kidnapper has her... Shit!"

I got up, knocking the little coffee table over, spilling the glasses, bottles, pieces of paper, crayons, and knickknacks loudly on the tiled floor.

"Colombe," Jerome said softly trying to grab me as I ran out of the room, tears streaming down my cheeks.

I ran out of the Lesueur's house to the end of their yard. Jerome joined me, hugging me, kissing me tenderly while rocking me gently. Little by little I calmed down.

"I can't do this anymore! It's too hard! Where is my sister? Is she still alive? We don't have one damn thing to help us find out where she'd being kept. Nothing! That other scumbag has been manipulating us for days now and playing games with us."

"We'll find him... Bertrand will be able to shed some light on those shadows, I'm sure of it. He seems to be pretty good at stuff like that."

"I sort of see him as our last hope."

"We have to keep on believing we'll find her, we can't give up. We don't have the right to. For Sara".

. . .

"For Sara."

CHAPTER 52
A nightmare-filled night

SARA, all curled up with her arms around her legs, was shivering. The room she'd been locked in for hours, perhaps even days, wasn't actually cold. But the fever she felt welling up in her head was what had sparked her shivering.

She didn't drink much, didn't eat enough to ease her hunger, and felt herself getting weaker hour by hour.

The foul smell of the urine that had pooled in a corner of the room and that permeated her slacks no longer bothered her. Gues you can get used to anything, including the worst.

She'd also got used to the light that filtered through the closed shutters on the tiny window in that room. At least she was able to distinguish night from day, have an idea of how many hours had gone by, draw up a crude mental calendar.

She thought she'd been there now for three days

and two nights. A tiny drop in her entire life, an eternity in such conditions.

During all this time, her jailkeeper had only come twice a day, to take away her empty bowls and give her full ones.

He barely spoke to her, she didn't dare ask him anything.

All she could hear from outside was a deafening silence, as if her prison was someplace at the end of the world, in a place deserted by humans. Every once in a while, she'd hear the indifferent chirping of a bird.

Sometimes, she could even see it through the tiny gaps in the shutters. The bird would land on the windowsill, shake, whistle a joyful melody, without caring the least for that tormented lady who was rotting inside.

That was her life now, her unique moment of mixed happiness and heartache: the song of that innocent jet-black little bird.

Up until the day he came back, but this time empty-handed. No bowls. Sara wondered if that was good or bad. She asked herself two questions.

Was he about to free her?

Or kill her?

The man walked towards her, his face still covered in a supple leather mask, with two holes for his nose, a hole for his mouth and two circles cut open where she could see his crazy eyes sparkling, though she was unable to distinguish their color.

He grabbed a folding chair that was up against the back wall and slowly unfolded it in the middle of the room.

He straddled it, his arms crossed on the backrest, turned towards Sara.

"How about a little chat? Wanna talk some?"

Sara nodded, preferring to remain silent. Let him say what he wanted to say and get it over with. One way of the other. As up till now, he hadn't seen fit to explain a single thing.

He continued.

"I'd imagine you've got loads of questions dancing around in your little head since you arrived. I bet you're wondering what you did to deserve punishment like this."

The young lady remained silent. She was staring at his eyes through his mask, trying to figure out who this unknown person was. Could two eyes give you an identity?

A range or specific tone of voice? A vague feeling of something familiar insinuated itself into Sara's ear. Not that she recognized that voice as one she could identify just with a few words on the phone for example. Yet there was a little something titillating her memory. Though she couldn't put her finger on any precise souvenir. She waited silently for him to speak more to try to have a clearer idea.

"My dear Sara, did you ever hear the expression *collateral damage*? Some people just don't have any luck. Those are words you often hear on the news. Like *there were a hundred victims in the bombing, blablabla..* Poor guys like just us who found themselves in the wrong place at the wrong time, under crossfire of two adversaries. A stray bullet... An unplanned and fatal consequence... See what I'm getting at? Do I blame you for it? Probably not... But... You were so easy to catch, so much fun too. You gotta laugh sometimes in life, don't you?"

The man made a noise between a snort and a laugh, sort of like a famished hyena in the Sahara Desert in the middle of the night. Sara quivered with fear while shivering in her cold urine-soaked pants.

"I can read in your eyes the questions you have. You're asking yourself: *Why me? Who is he? Where did he come from? What does he want from me? Why did he do that? Where are we? What's he going to do to me? Will I ever see my daughter again?*"

As the masked man was ticking down his chaplet of questions, the young lady was nodding while putting her hands against her ears. Trying to flee reality. Escape mentally. But sitting right across from her jailer's inquisitive eyes, she had no other solution than to listen to his monologue.

"To answer all, or at least most of these legitimate questions, I'm going to tell you a story. Okay? You wanna hear it? Even if you don't I'm still going to tell it. All you have to do is to imagine that it's a nice little story you're telling a child to help them fall asleep. I know, it's not going to be easy. Ready? Take your hands off your ears!"

As Sara didn't obey, the man suddenly jumped up from his chair and approached her, threatening, with that riding crop she knew only too well as the end of his arm.

She screamed, took her hands off her ears and shook her head up and down, several times.

"Alright. That's better."

He walked back to his chair, straddled it and began his tale.

"This is a tale of a teen," the masked man begun. "A perturbed adolescence. That's probably a euphemism... everyone went through that thankless age. It's the story about a young boy who didn't feel good about himself, like most teens, but for him it was worse, or stronger you could say. A boy who was secretly in love with a young girl, a beautiful and gracious one. That girl, he couldn't get her out of his mind. Except he was never able to touch her, to approach her. That proud girl had no idea. He didn't even exist for her. He was no one. Between those two, any intimate relationships were impossible. So that young boy got frustrated, tense, and angry. He lost himself, in his head, his body, his soul. He wasn't going to sell his soul to the devil, like the saying goes. No, that soul, it would simply crack, slowly, inexorably, up until it was torn apart. As you know, when you're a teenager, you search for your real self. Sometimes you find it, other times you don't. He didn't. He looked for his salvation elsewhere, as that girl didn't want him, no other girls wanted him even, he was hopeless. So anyway, he looked around and found a way to console himself, out of frustration, with a friend who had already found his way. So, what was bound to happen happened. He crossed the yellow line, he went through the looking glass, you get it? He was no longer the same boy, that was for sure, and it was irreversible. Hey! Don't fall asleep on me!"

Sara, lulled by her guardian's logorrhea and exhausted, felt her eyelids closing rapidly.

"You're not interested in my story? It should remind you of something. Doesn't it?"

The young lady refused to accept that idea.

"Okay. Let me continue, we'll soon be at the last chapters. But not the epilogue... So anyway, that now transformed young man was going to see things go downhill fast for him. His new sexual preference didn't please the other guys, the real ones, those who chug beer, watch football and fuck girls. For them, he's introverted, a fag, a homo. As of then, he'd become their scapegoat. And his life would brutally turn into a living hell. Want me to tell you how?"

"No," Sara sobbed.

"I'm gonna tell you anyway. After that, you'll understand. So one day, actually one night, there was a party in one of the teenager's houses in town. A nice house, one with a pool. A rich family, parents who had left for the weekend, teens all alone. That night, everything changed for him. A nightmare scenario... Just listen."

CHAPTER 53
Scorching tears

Summer 2008

AT THE END OF JULY, *some high school students heard the scuttlebutt, and the rumor began to spread at school, bursting like a bubble on a bar of soap.*

"There's that fairy..."

"That's a no-brainer, ugly like he is, there's no way a girl would look at him twice."

"Come on you dumb ass! Ever look at yourself? Who do you think you are to judge people like that?"

"Me? I'm a stud, wanna check?"

"Still with his pimple face, you can tell he's queer."

The rumors grew, from group to group, with jibes openly given. In just a couple of weeks, that ostracizing phenomenon grew, until it created a deleterious and shunning atmosphere.

Pointed at, he began to cut himself off from the world, lost in his misunderstood desires. He intrinsically

— unless it was culturally — felt attracted by girls, but no longer knew how to take the first step, maybe he'd never known.

His grades began to drop, his mood degenerated, and he plunged a bit more into those easy and guilt-ridden relations.

Till the day when everything changed.

A SUMMER EVENING that started out like all the summer evenings in a house that cool parents left to their supposedly responsible offspring. It was still hot around that pool lit up by blue, green and orange lights. Music was blaring, games were being played, beer and cocktails were being downed. Teens were swimming, diving, splashing. Dancing and singing. Guys eyeing girls, girls eying guys, they formed little groups, then couples who squatted a couch, or went in a different room, or found a spare bed. Kissing, necking, and more.

Hours went by, their alcohol content soared, tempers flared.

Some were having the time of their lives, others not so much. The repressed pimply faced teen was in the second group. To overcome his fear and unhappiness, he drank more than he should have. A few joints were being passed around, he didn't turn them down either. Taking that all into account, he was a bit more than wheezy and out of it, as were most of those at the party that evening.

So when a handful of them, the most extroverted ones, encircled him next to the pool, he hadn't the energy to try to shake them off. Night had fallen ages ago, stars were twinkling in that dark sky, it was now cool without being cold. In his head however, things were boiling, his forehead was throbbing. Those guys started yelling at him, but he was having trouble understanding what they wanted.

"So, cocksucker, you like big ones?"

"Fuck off," he managed to retort.

"That's the way he talks to us? You hear that?"

"Hey there! Who the hell do you think you are?"

He felt them lifting him under his armpits, one guy on each side, carting him off. A glimmer of lucidity made him hope they wouldn't throw him in the pool. In his state, he'd probably sink, especially as he was still in his street clothes. No one paid any attention to them at the poolside, everyone was just having fun, the music was blaring.

For him though, the party was over.

The four men *were like a bulwark surrounding him.*

"You dicklicker, we're gonna have some fun. There's a shed over there."

And in the back of the yard there was a little wooden shed that looked like a gardener's shed.

One of them pushed the door, which wasn't locked. They dragged him inside. He tried to resist, call for help, but one of them put his hand over his mouth.

"Shut the fuck up! No one can hear you anyway. So

you just be a good little boy till we decide what to do with you."

"What do..."

A loud clout on his face shut him up, sending his glasses off someplace and triggering a sharp ringing in his right ear.

"I told you to shut up!"

That blow though had quickly sobered him up. Enough anyway to enable him to understand what those four guys, quite athletic ones — guys he'd seen at school but never hung out with — were intending to do to him. There was a sturdy oak table in the middle of the shed. Sneering like lustful hyenas, that's where they dragged him.

He tried to fight them off, but the others were holding him down so firmly that his wrists and his neck ached.

"You lay down there!"

They forced him to lie on his stomach brutally. His cheek hit the wood, he could see its marbled veins patinated by time. That table must have been at least a hundred years old, he even for a fleeting moment wondered when it was made. That quickly though became the least of his concerns when one of them pulled his jeans down to his ankles. He was now fettered, unable to struggle or move. Lying on the table, his hips against the angle, two guys were holding his arms out on each side.

He yelled for help. One more clout.

"Shut up!"

Someone stuffed a rag into his mouth.

"Go ahead, try again, see if you can!"

He didn't bother, he understood that he couldn't. Heat began to mount in his face, heat that quickly turned into scorching tears running down his cheeks.

"Pull that bitch's pants down."

He felt his cotton boxers being pulled down and a fresh breeze on his nude buttocks. He was paralyzed by a mixture of shame and fear.

"He doesn't look like much from the front, but that pig does have a nice little butt! Almost like a girl's butt, don't you think so guys? He doesn't even have any hair. Who wants to start? I'm sure it's gonna go in like butter and he'll love it."

"Yeah, well why don't you go first, all that looks pretty tight to me and I don't feel like busting my Johnson going in."

"Just wait, we'll see what we can do."

He heard them rummaging around in the shed. Drawers were being opened, objects clinking together, metal against wood.

He suddenly felt something cold on his buttocks. He anus contracted itself as a reflex.

"Spit on it, we don't want to hurt the poor pussy."

He suddenly felt a searing pain penetrating him. His thighs trembled with the shock, his stomach contracted, his eye popped open by surprise at first, and then by the burning pain. His flesh screamed though the rag in his mouth prevented him from calling for help again. He jerked around like some poor frog being tortured by sadistic little kids, but as his arms were being held, his ankles immobilized, he was powerless, at the mercy of his torturers.

"There you go. It's in. People always say the first inch is the hardest, after that it's just something you get used to," one of them said mockingly. "Now that the coast is clear, we can go in!"

"Why don't you start, yours is the smallest. Might as well increase in size, if not it won't be any fun."

"Hey! Screw you! At least I ain't got the limpest one..."

"So show us what you can do then, gnome nuts!"

The victim could have cared less about that debate. He had to try to extract himself mentally from that abject moment. He had no other choice, he squeezed everything he could: his teeth, his eyes, everything. The guys all took turns. One after the other, the four laughing and mocking guys. One of them, hung like a donkey, ripped him apart.

He was incapable of counting how many minutes, who knows, how many hours had gone by, he'd lost track of time. His entire body had become a mass of aching flesh, the pain permeated his body along his backbone each time they rammed him.

Then it was over. His legs could barely support him. He felt a hot liquid dripping down his thighs.

That was when he passed out.

CHAPTER 54
Tracks of its prey

ANOTHER NIGHT WENT BY, in slow motion. Each minute without any news of my sister, without any leads or details about where she could be, was like an hour to us.

Since our wedding day, we'd been despite ourselves, competing in a race against the clock, a race against time, organized by the author of those threats and Sara's kidnapper. Like he'd said, it was now a race against death. My sister's death? Someone else close to us?

What was most important was finding Sara. In the morning, after an umpteenth sleepless night, we finally had a lead. A bit of blue sky that Bertrand, who had spent the whole night staring at his screens, his keyboards, his mouse, told me.

"Hey cuz', it's Bert. I gotta admit this morning I'm squinting pretty bad, because I didn't close my eyes for the whole night. I worked for you, and I think I might have something. I still have to see if we can exploit it or not. There's still a couple of things I have to check, two or three elements to crosscheck and it should work. But I just wanted you to know that things are going in the right direction. I thought you'd like to hear something a little bit positive, a little ray of sun breaking through your cloudy sky."

"Thanks so much. That really means a lot to me. So you found something then?"

"Hold your horses! I'm going to describe the method I used to draw my conclusions. I do have a margin for error because I'm sure you're not going to appreciate the conclusion I arrived at. You remember that I told you that messages like these, sent from the dark web were almost untraceable?"

"Yes, I do. But *almost* doesn't mean *completely*."

"That's it. And there are ways to bypass the different anonymous layers, untie connection knots and hack the servers that were used to send the messages."

"That's Greek for me. Pretend I'm five years old."

"Okay then, to put it in images, let's just say that I was able to enter in clandestinely in the cars that transported the messages to your cell phones, emails, cloud and all that. And what I feared the most at the beginning was true, meaning that the guy was very careful, including physically so. What I mean is that he didn't just protect himself virtually, but he also sent out his messages from public spots using his own computer of course, in cafes, train stations, airports, places where they had Wi-Fi networks. So we can't find out where he lives. Plus he moved around. He sent some from Bordeaux, some from Marseille, another time from the middle of France. A rascal who doesn't like to stay put. Someone who's not afraid to drive for miles to cover his tracks. But I'm not astonished by that."

I was beginning to chomp at the bit here with everything Bertrand had told me and explained.

"Spit it out Bert! So your deductions, where did they lead you?"

"To an elementary question. What kind of people move in just a few days around the country. What kind of professions are frequent travelers, or travel for long distances? For me, pointblank, I'd say a truck driver, for example. Or someone who drives a train. Or a pilot. Or a salesman covering a large geographical sector."

"Or a taxi driver," I added, thinking about the one who had driven Grandma Suzanne to her room in the residence and who had also driven us to Merignac Airport.

One of the only people who knew we were going to Marseille.

Clearly it looked like that guy was following us.

I told Bertrand about that omnipresent taxi driver and that made him react.

"Do you have his phone number or his email? Anything?"

"Wait a second, he gave me his business card."

I found it in my purse and gave Bertrand the taxi driver's cell phone number.

"Great! I got my work cut out for me in the next few hours. I'll do it as quickly as possible."

"Did you tell Delahousse about your hypotheses?"

"I'll give him a call. But before that, I'm going to go over your guest list and try to crosscheck the locations of their cell phones. See if any of them overlap with places where those anonymous messages were sent. This could lead us to the designated victim or to Sara's kidnapper. Anyway, if it works, it's over for him! I'll call you back!"

Bertrand hung up without another word, undoubtedly excited just like a hound dog sniffing the tracks of its prey.

CHAPTER 55
Music soothes the savage beast

THINGS FINALLY SEEMED to be looking up for us. We thought we at least had a lead. I told Damien and Jerome about what Bertrand had talked about. They both hoped that we'd soon have a favorable outcome. We were all slightly relieved, and because of that significant reduction in tension, were all suddenly exhausted.

That didn't last long though, as we all had a new message in our inboxes.

From the usual person, the author of our torments, once again torturing us.

From: Anonymousemail

Subject: Music soothes the savage beast

. . .

There was no text in the message. Just a simple mp4 file that I clicked on.

The file was sent into my downloads file, and I could see it charging. When the process was finished, the audio app of my phone automatically opened, and I could hear the first notes.

I remember a tree, I remember the wind
   Those rumors of waves in the endless ocean
   I remember a city, I remember a voice
   From those Christmases shining in the snow and the cold
   I remember a dream, I remember a king
   Of a summer that's ending, of a house made from wood
   I remember the sky, I remember the water
   A lace dress that was ripped in back
   Blood isn't what runs through our veins
   It's the river of our childhood
   Death isn't what saddens me
   It's that I can no longer see my father dancing...

The song suddenly cut off.

I pressed the mp4 icon once again and the song began from the beginning.

Then stopped at the same place.

"You think it's an infected file? Try it on your phone," I asked Jerome.

My husband did the same thing I had, and the same thing happened to him.

"Sometimes files haven't been sent correctly and they lose data in the transmission process," Damien suggested.

"No, I think it was done intentionally. I'm starting to know this guy," I replied. "I'm sure he wanted to cut the song off right then, because that was what he wanted. As usual, he's conveying a message to us."

"Start it up again so we can pay attention to the lyrics."

Which was what I did, scrutinizing each sentence, each word, right up till that last chilling sentence, the one with all those innuendos.

Death isn't what saddens me
It's that I can no longer see my father dancing...

My father, who I danced with at our wedding right after I'd opened the ball with Jerome.

"NOOOO!" I screamed. "That can't be! Is this ever going to stop? After my sister, my father?"

I quickly scrolled through my contacts list on my phone. I wanted to find my father's number right away but caught a bad case of moist fat fingers. I opened one application mistakenly, closed another one, panicking.

"Calm down, hun," Jerome said to me.

"How can you ask me to calm down when my father's maybe the next victim?"

I finally phoned him, but as usual, he didn't

answer. He often didn't have his phone on him, forgot it here or there, in the house, in his car, in a jacket he'd worn a couple of days ago. Or the battery was dead. I didn't bother leaving him a message, he'd never listen to it anyway, and I phoned my mom. Too bad if I'd have to tell her about what we were going through. It was too serious to have any consideration. My parents — who of course were also Sara's parents — would die from anxiety and apprehension and I insidiously felt guilty for making them go through that. Guilty of leaving them in ignorance up till now, guilty of not telling them their oldest daughter was missing. I'd said to myself that it was to protect them, but I was undoubtedly wrong.

I could no longer back away from what had happened, that triple threat on our family.

Those anonymous messages saying they'd kill one of the guests at our wedding…

Sara's kidnapping.

The last message that seemed to target my father.

My mother picked up on the third ringtone. I barged right in, out of breath.

"Mom, you have to listen to me without interrupting. Is dad with you?"

"No, he left about two hours ago to walk in the forest, like he does every day. Why?"

I quickly told my mom all about the letters and everything, all the details, so she'd realize how upset I was about my dad's absence.

"Jesus Christ, honey! That's horrible. And of

course your dad left his phone here as usual. I keep telling him to take it with him! You know he has heart problems and I'm always afraid that something will happen when he goes out walking like that. I keep on telling him, but he'll never change, that idiot!"

"Mom, that's not the problem. We have to inform the police. I'll do it. And we're coming over."

"But you're on the other side of the country."

In my precipitation, I'd forgotten that Provence, in the southeast of France, is quite far away from Landes, on the west coast.

"I don't give a damn! I'm not going to stay here doing nothing when my dad is maybe the next person on the list... After Grandma, Sara... We have to stop this crazy man!"

And with Jerome and Damien, that's what we decided to do. Our brother-in-law also agreed with us, hoping that he'd find his wife at the same time. *Why not kill two birds with one stone,* he added.

Damien rushed over to his neighbor's house to ask her to babysit Justine, as he often did when Sara and he went to the movies or to the restaurant. As her daughter was Justine's best friend, the young lady accepted without asking too many questions. It's important to have good neighbors.

We packed as quickly as possible and started off, towards the setting sun, in my brother-in-law's car. His hands were gripping the steering wheel tensely, betraying his anxiety as well as his determination to do something, just like us.

As we were speeding down the highway towards Bordeaux, my mom called.

"He's back! Your dad's at home. I bawled him out for scaring us like that! I'm sure he'll never forget his phone again."

I was relieved and thanked my mother for having called us.

So, if my father was safe and sound, who was the target of that threat in the song?

While we were driving, we listened to that song again on my phone.

Even more attentively this time.

Suddenly there was a light that went on in my brain.

I understood what the lyrics of that song were hiding and why he'd chosen them. I understood the hidden and yet so evident meaning.

A meaning that brought harrowing memories that had been hidden deep down inside.

CHAPTER 56
To be someone different

LEANING OVER HIS KEYBOARDS, looking from one screen to another, his fingers feverishly typing away, Bertrand felt as if he had been sucked into an emotional spiral and couldn't get out of it. He checked for the umpteenth time all that sensitive data to make sure he hadn't made a mistake, but he trusted his computers and the software he'd installed in them. The technology that his investigations were based on.

The result of that ultimate verification confirmed his recent hypotheses, that had stemmed from the many cross-checks he'd carried out. On the wall across from him, he'd thumbtacked several sheets of paper on which he'd scribbled various diagrams that had a multitude of names, dates, and places linked together by lines.

He couldn't doubt it anymore, his theory was right.

. . .

He sighed loudly and picked up his phone.

"Hey, Bertrand. You got something new? Your computers found something?"

Colombe's voice had a distant echo.

"You're in the car?"

"That's right. We're going to Thiezac. I'll explain it to you. But what did you find? It's the taxi driver, isn't it?"

Bertrand didn't answer immediately.

"That's right... the taxi driver."

"Holy crap! And just think we were in his car the other day. We had him... or he had us. Why didn't we understand earlier?"

"Wait a sec, cuz. Calm down. I'm telling you it *is* the taxi driver, just maybe not the one you thought it was."

"What are you talking about? How many taxi drivers are there?"

"Thousands of them in France! Just let me continue! So. I was able to trace the movements of the taxi driver you told me about, using a variety of cross-checks that I won't go into detail about. Stuff with networks, GPS, etc. Anyway, though some of the positions correspond, they don't overlap in the different places that concern us. Amongst others, your driver hasn't set foot in Marseille for ages. So I'd say that we can rule him out of your list of suspects. Or else he has several accomplices, which would make things more complicated. What I can tell you though is that I spent hours scoping out all your wedding guests and hang on here, there's one person whose movements and IP addresses correspond perfectly to the anonymous messages."

"Spit it out! Who?"

"Listen, and I know this is completely crazy and even I found it hard to believe the results, though I double-checked them several times. I don't know if you want to hear his name…"

"Jeez Louise, Bertrand! Of course I do! Stop torturing me! Go ahead!"

"Okay. But what I'm going to tell you isn't pretty… It's someone in the family…"

"Bertrand! This isn't funny!"

"No, it's not. Without any doubt at all, the author of those anonymous messages you've been getting for days now, and the person who kidnapped Sara in Verdon… is our cousin Pascal."

"Pascal?"

"That's right. Pascal. Who was at your wedding. With whom you laughed, maybe even danced. Who was with you at our chamber pot ritual. Colombe, you have no idea how sorry I am to have to be the one telling you that. I would have liked it to be someone different. But I owe you the truth, and that's it."

It was silent at the other end of the line. Colombe was holding her head in her hands, her eyes closed and moist. She thought about one of the sentences in that poem.

"The solution is hidden closer than you may actually believe," she droned on.

"Huh?"

"It's nothing. Pascal, someone close. My own cousin. This whole clusterfuck is a family affair then? Why though? And to think that I completely forgot that Pascal was a taxi driver... Had I thought of that earlier, maybe Sara's kidnapping could have been avoided. But I can't understand his intentions. What does he want with Sara? Why is he targeting her?"

"Stop torturing yourself Colombe. It's not the moment for regrets, it's time for action."

"What do you think we should do?"

"I've got Pascal's geolocalization data. And I'm sure you're not going to be surprised at where he is. Right now he's near Aurillac. At Thiezac more precisely. Ring a bell?"

"Of course it does," Colombe replied. "Totally. And that is exactly where we're headed."

CHAPTER 57
Moaning

HE TURNED his vehicle off and stopped his taximeter. The day was over for Pascal Claussade, he worked hard to make a living.

He got out of his cab, locked the doors and went into his house.

As soon as he opened the door he heard whining and whimpering.

"Jesus Christ!" he complained, throwing his keys on the sideboard. "She can't shut up?"

He hung his jacket up and walked up to the door where those sounds were coming from. He quickly opened it and jogged downstairs, taking them two by two, rushing to that shadow which instinctively curled up in a corner, moaning weakly.

"What the fuck is wrong now?" shouted Pascal when he saw the bowls that were tipped over, their content on the floor. "Plus it stinks to high heaven here! If only I had known what trouble you'd be here.

Okay, come on, we're going for a little walk both of us. You need some fresh air. We'll see where that'll take us."

He untied and unfettered her.

They went outside in the dark, with only a few weak moonbeams lighting them up.

CHAPTER 58
Rumors of waves

CLOSE. When we were kids, Pascal and I were close. Maybe we didn't really hang out together, but we were cousins, of course with our parents we often saw each other.

Close. We weren't geographically close though. That's life. I'd left our childhood village, and he'd stayed.

Close, we were close physically on the day Jerome and I got married.

Close. How could we remain close when he was playing with our nerves, our lives?

We were driving as quickly as possible towards Thiezac, to be close one last time.

Before separating permanently, one way or the other.

I listened once again to that song by Garou and Michel Sardou. Things were now clearer.

. . .

*I remember a **tree**, I remember the **wind***
*Those **rumors** of **waves** in the endless ocean*
*I remember a city, I remember a **voice***
*Of **a summer that's ending**, of a house made from wood*
*I remember the **sky**, I remember the **water***
*A **lace dress** that was ripped in back*
***Blood** isn't what runs through our veins*
*It's the river of our **childhood***

In my mind, some of the words sung by that duo of French-speaking artists were blinking just like warning lights. Keywords that could only refer to one thing: that river where all of us always hung out when we were teenagers. The place we sometimes stayed at for the entire day, or where we spent our evenings with a campfire, roasting hot dogs and marshmallows, or where we sometimes even camped out. The place where our budding adult lives began. All sorts of shows took place there. Comedies, vaudeville, burlesque, tragicomedies, but drama too?

Between friends, between siblings, between cousins.

Though I still didn't really get what that venue meant, I was sure that it was the place that Pascal was referring to. That had to be true, too many points sharing coincidences were coming together here at that symbolic venue of our teenaged years.

Would we find Sara prisoner there? Was that a trap

or an illusion? Could we trust the clues Pascal had given us? Were we going to throw ourselves into the lion's den?

Yet despite that new litany of questions, we had no other solution than to go to Thiezac, on the banks of the Pas de Cere, the place where we'd spent so many days when we were growing up.

It was still a couple of hours' drive away, and Jerome, Damien and I all took turns at the wheel.

When we turned into the village, I had a twinge of sorrow in my heart. I hadn't been back there for at least ten years after I'd migrated down to Nice to go to journalism school.

"Turn right, at that roundabout," I told Damien who now was driving. "After the stoplight, keep on going straight about five hundred feet, then you turn left."

I guided him until we crossed the bridge. *The* bridge. Under which we lit our campfires. Where we hid to avoid indiscreet eyes to put on or take off our bathing suits. Under which we smoked our first cigarettes or illicit substances.

The one that was *the river of our childhood*.

Damien parked his car on the roadside right after that stone bridge, pointing its headlights towards the little grassy path descending gently to the river's banks.

Everything was thus lit up by those two white headlights shining in the night with a shadowy halo.

I looked down at what we'd fondly called "our beach." Which unsurprisingly was deserted. Or at least from the bridge we couldn't see anyone.

"No one," I regretted contritely.

"What were you expecting?" Damien asked. "A marching band? Trumpets, banners and confetti? Pascal wearing a tux with outstretched arms?"

"You're right", I admitted. "Let's get out."

I got out first, followed by Jerome and Damien right behind me, though on the lookout. I could hear the peaceful tiny waves of the river lapping on the pebbled beach. Looking down through the axis of the headlights once again led us to the same conclusion: no one was there.

"Turn your phone lamps on," suggested Jerome. "Let's have a look under the bridge."

There was no light from the moon nor from the headlights under the bridge, a mysterious semi-darkness. And if?

Nearly in unison, our phone lights lit up the space between the two pillars holding up the bridge, with a bright, crude and surgical-type of light. We then saw the reality.

It was also deserted.

"Shit. Maybe we got it all wrong," I hesitated. "What did I miss? Did we jump right into a trap? He was waving a decoy in front of us?"

I mentally hummed the lyrics of the song, one that

I now knew by heart, as I sat down on the beach. I was exhausted. Exhausted by days of anxiety and nights of insomnia. Exhausted by thinking all the time. Exhausted by that ominous impression that we'd never find Sara alive again.

I suddenly had a flash.

*I remember a **tree**, I remember the wind...*

THAT WAS IT! That several centuries-old tree, the one that dominated all the others with its high canopy and in which the wind blew its romantic melodies.

That tree whose bark had had to endure countless febrile knives leaving memories of love stories we thought would never end.

That tree at the foot of which there was a cranny, making it an ideal hiding place for squirrels' nuts.

Or for tender little love letters...

No one could forget such a tree.

I got back up quickly, full of new hope and ran towards the oak tree in question, using the light from my phone. I went into the cluster of trees next to the river.

"Colombe!" shouted Jerome in my back. "Wait for us! Where are you going?"

Obsessed with my goal, I didn't bother answering him.

With a few careful footsteps so as not to fall because of the airy roots, but not paying any attention to the brambles and holes in the earth, I arrived at the foot of the tree.

I kneeled down in front of the hole. Nothing had changed, except perhaps the thickness of the moss whose odor of humus tickled my nostrils. Something that reminded me of cemeteries.

I put my hand into the cavity. With the other, I held my phone, trying to light up its dark depths.

My fingers felt a smooth, cold and visibly plasticized surface. I picked it up.

It was a plastic pouch with a sheet of paper inside and another object that I didn't immediately identify.

I opened it and squealed with fright.

CHAPTER 59
A tacky brown substance

THE PIECE of paper contained in that waterproof pouch, rolled up like a parchment, was covered with quite an inelegant handwriting. Poorly written letters that must either have been written much too hastily or by someone half crazy. I was able though to make out one of the sentences, which was a verse of the song, *Our Childhood River*, the one that he led us here.

A summer drawing to an end in a house made from wood, where *a house made from wood* had been underlined twice, furiously, like a cutter had slashed twice through that nominal group.

I had trouble making out what followed, as the letters trembled, danced, were poorly linked or on the other hand, all indistinctly mixed together.

I could distinguish a few snippets though.

C*olombe*, *do you remember a sweet summer's night?*

... in your swimsuit that didn't hide your...
... lit up pool... music... laughter... alcohol... joints... a marvelous and unforgettable evening?
I screamed, you didn't hear anything.
... could have saved...
... completely abandoned that night in the...
... branded for life... because of you...
... hidden inside me for too long... time to pay... that night...

To read every word I would have had to examine the document carefully to decipher its meaning. But we didn't have time, it was now time to act. We had to save Sara who had been kidnapped by Pascal. That cousin who had suffered when he was a teen, if what his last letter, a type of confession, was true.

A letter that I had to interpret by reading between the lines. But those little snippets of sentences sparked memories I had forgotten for ages. I know that memory is a mystery, an iffy thing, one that sometimes takes sinuous paths. It sometimes allows your memories to flee, other times it stores them someplace so you will be able to remember them at a later date, one day or another, depending on the specific conditions.

And here the conditions were conducive to that boomerang memory effect. I had forgotten that party at the end of summer 2008 for the simple reason that for me, it was just like all the other parties I'd gone to. On the other hand, I now realized that for other people, including Pascal, that night and party had been horrible, though I had no idea what could have happened nor why.

An uncurable and overwhelming pain.

One he had to express by hook or by crook, even years later.

I was beginning to apprehend the source of his pain and especially his bitterness though I had no idea how Sara could have been involved in it.

Or not yet I should have said. We'd learn that a bit later when we'd find where he was hiding my sister.

Something I now understood, by crossing Pascal's clues with my memories as a teenager.

The pool, heavy drinking, the music and that *house made from wood*.

I was still kneeling down facing the tree, curled up, the wrinkled sheet of paper in my hand, hot tears pouring silently down my cheeks.

"Honey, what is it?" asked Jerome in a gentle and soothing voice, kneeling behind me, his hands on my shoulders.

I was shaking so hard I couldn't articulate a single word, buried in a mountain of souvenirs like a pile of fallen leaves or damp moss.

Through my moist eyes, I looked at the object that the waterproof pouch Pascal had hidden in the hole under the tree also contained. An uninteresting object, though it made me quiver.

An object that looked like a removable handle of a frying pan. Something totally ordinary you'd find in any kitchen and that wouldn't be terrifying in other circumstances.

But that was when you didn't look at what it had on one of its ends. That handle was covered with a tacky brown substance, one that looked like dried blood to me.

"Don't touch that!" implored Jerome when he saw my hand approaching it.

"Sara…" I trembled. "No, not that!"

"Come here, we've got to get going. Time is of the essence. Tell us what that makes you think of."

I could tell them, but I wasn't capable of uttering a word. Too overwhelmed by what that could mean, both in the past and in the present. I made an effort, mentally shaking myself.

"I think I know what wooden house he's referring to."

"Where is it?" Damien asked. With Jerome's assistance, he helped me get up.

I felt so empty, so weak. All of those days with their accumulated stress had suddenly undermined both my determination and my strength. But I couldn't give up now, we had to find my sister safe and sound and rescue her. I'd have time to rest later on. Sleep for a whole week if I needed to.

In the meanwhile though, I had to keep my eyes open and focus.

"I remember a party end of the summer in 2008

here in the village. One of the girls in my class had rich parents and a huge house and they often let us use it without any supervision. There was a pool, a big yard with lots of trees in it, and at the back of the yard there was this wooden shed. You know, something that a gardener could use, or a hunter, it was pretty big actually for a shed and quite a few people could fit in. Anyway, there were quite a few hormone-filled teens there that night, everyone had been drinking, dreaming of sex, no adults were there, anything would have been possible."

"So where's that house then?" Jerome asked impatiently.

"At the end of the village, when you're driving towards Vic-sur-Cere."

"And you think he's trying to lure us there?"

"I'm sure of it."

"Let's get going then, we can't waste any more time."

CHAPTER 60
Primary instincts

AS HE WAS WALKING BACK HOME, Pascal Claussade had the vague impression that someone was spying on him. After an hour's walk with his rescue dog who'd been tugging on his leash the whole time, Pascal was glad to be back home.

When he'd taken in that abandoned dog a couple of weeks ago, he was sure he was making a mistake but couldn't resist. He'd done some research on the web and had concluded that the animal was a female American Staffordshire Terrier, a dog people often referred to as a Staff, one that was wrongly considered to be one of the most dangerous ones in the world. A sweet and friendly dog, but one that had it been abused or trained to fight, could be aggressive and attack, with its primary instincts revealing themselves in a sort of post-traumatic stress disorder.

He'd discovered the wounded dog in an industrial brown zone, and the animal had allowed Pascal to pick it up and put it in his taxi, after he'd finished his work that evening.

Back home, so he wouldn't bother his neighbors, Pascal decided to lock the dog in his basement where his barking or whining would be attenuated.

Pascal was a workaholic. A fare was a fare, a buck was a buck, and you had to add a maximum of them together in a day, week, month to make money. Then after paying for gas, social contributions and taxes, there wasn't much of that hard-earned money left over to splurge. The young thirty-year-old worked as long as he could and was away from his home most of the time, leaving his Staff chained up in the basement all day long. He brought food and water to his dog in the morning and evening. He usually waited until it was dark outside to walk the dog, who needed exercise and tugged on its leash with all her strength.

THE MAN and his dog were nearing his home when suddenly headlights came on about fifty feet away, pointed right at him, making it hard for him to see anything.

Pascal raised his forearm to his eyes to protect them from that blinding light and his Staff began to growl, her snout pointed at the vehicle, her chops raised, baring her pointed fangs.

"Stay where you are!" shouted a voice from behind that luminous halo. "Police!"

The young man was petrified.

He saw three shadows moving carefully towards him and his dog. Three men with square shoulders, their arms pointed straight at him.

"What the fuck is going on here?"

"Raise your hands and don't let your dog loose."

"I didn't do anything. I pay my taxes, I declare everything, I'm an honest citizen," Pascal defended himself.

"We're sure you are. That's not why we're here. Calm down."

The closer the three policemen were, the more the dog began to growl and bark. She was tugging on her leash as if she wanted to attack those three shadows, something that must have sparked memories in that battered animal's brain.

"Shut that dog up! If it escapes, I'm shooting it!"

Those Chinese shadows were now within six feet of the dog and its owner.

"Do you have a doghouse or someplace you can put that mutt?" asked one of the cops brusquely.

"In my basement," Pascal stammered.

"We'll follow you. You lock that monster up and after that we can talk calmly."

"Talk about what? What did I do?"

"You'll know soon enough."

The police escorted Pascal into his home. He locked his dog in his basement, under the vigilant eyes of the policemen who quickly inspected the rest of his house. Then they interrogated him, leaving him dumbfounded, incredulous and surprised to find out what they thought he'd done.

Later on, the chief of the police called one of his colleagues in charge of the investigation.

"Captain Delahousse? Agent Becker here. We just left the home of that Pascal Claussade. A dead end, nothing there."

CHAPTER 61
Life-threatening

WE ARRIVED at the house where that party had taken place, the one where dozens of teens were left to their own devices, at risk of generating terrible abuse. Which is what must have happened fifteen years ago, exactly back in 2008.

I immediately recognized the premises, though I hadn't set foot there for ages. Some places let's just say you never forget them.

The tall walls surrounding the property made it impossible for anyone outside to see what was going on there. A huge wrought iron gate closed access to the driveway.

Damien, Jerome and I got out of the car, in front of the gate. Behind its heavy bars, we saw a sorry sight. There were brambles, tall grasses and trees that hadn't been cut for years, mixed in with a few sad and confused flowers. That was when we saw a sign, one we hadn't paid any attention to at first.

. . .

For Sale

"You're sure this is the place?" asked Damien.

"One hundred percent. It's the only place like this in town."

At first we were afraid we wouldn't be able to get in or climb the wall, but then we saw that the chain that linked the two wings of the gate didn't have a lock on it. It was on the ground, on the other side of the gate, and in all likelihood someone had used a bolt cutter to cut it open. All we had to do was to push one of the gates that opened in a rusty squeak in the night lit up only by our cell phones.

"It's a sign," I predicted. "Let's go in." If my memories were right, that wooden shed was someplace in the back.

"We should wait for the cops," Damien said.

"Sure, with our arms dangling while he kills Sara?" I railed. "Do what you want, I'm going in. My sister's life is in danger."

Jerome went in front of me.

"I don't think so. I think on the contrary, that he wants to play with us and wants us to go to him. Which makes me think there's no life-threatening danger for your sister. From a psychological point of view, he needs us to come to deliver his message. Had he wanted to kill her, she'd already be dead, and we'd know about it, he'd give us some proof... Instead of that, he's dropping clues left, right and center, to lead us here, to witness his triumph. That's what I think, anyway."

My eyes filled with rage, I pulled away from my husband and took off in the darkness, relying on the bit of moonlight coming through the clouds from that large waxing moon. The soles of my shoes squeaked on the grass-filled gravel.

Jerome sprinted to join me.

"Colombe! Wait a second, don't do anything foolish!"

"Married only a week and you're already running after your wife!" Damien, behind everyone, tried to joke.

Nervous like we all were, he could have said anything.

After having run for about nine hundred feet, I saw that wooden shed quite clearly. Its shutters were closed, but you could see beams of light coming through their gaps. I was sure they were there. We had finally ended that crazy race against death that a sick cousin had conceived.

Out of breath, I stopped about ten feet from the front door, my hands on my knees, my heart pounding in my chest. Jerome was there immediately whereas Damien, quite out of shape, had to walk up to us.

We were sure that our footsteps on the gravel must have been heard and that Pascal must now have been aware of our presence, if he was inside with Sara, as his last message had led us to believe.

Damien finally caught up with us and before we could do anything he ran up to the shed and began pounding on its door. He was furious!

"Sara! Sara!"

He tried to break the door down with his shoulder. For the first time in several hours, my brother-in-law's apathy was finished. Since his wife had gone missing, he'd experienced roughly every negative emotion possible: incomprehension, wrath, shame, despair, despondency, and now that determination to end this all.

A determination that Jerome and I both shared, also trying to enter the shed. We shook the shutters and ran around the building looking for a way in.

From inside, we heard a cynical laugh.

Then the muffled voice, one I'd recognize anywhere, of my sister.

Sara was alive!

My phone then vibrated. Captain Delahousse was trying to reach me at this time of the night. I answered it, my hands trembling.

"Mrs. Bastaro. My men saw your cousin Pascal Claussade at his home, but didn't find any trace of your sister and he seems to be totally innocent."

"But, in that case, who kidnapped Sara?"

. . .

"Make sure you don't try anything alone," ordered Delahousse. "I'll be there soon with a team from Thiezac."

While we were driving here, I'd sent him a quick text message telling him where we were heading. We could now hope that the police force would come help us, but at this point, we couldn't dilly-dally anymore. We'd decided to take the risk of entering into that shed alone, without waiting for them. That's where Sara was, between those four wooden walls. We had to deliver her ask quickly as possible from the claws of her jailer.

I hung up.

"Who is in there?" I whispered, not understanding a thing.

Damien and Jerome kept pounding on the door.

Suddenly, between two blows, we heard a mocking voice, a parody of Charles Perrault and his fairy tale, *Little Red Riding Hood*.

"*Pull the bobbin, and the latch will go up!*"

"Asshole!" my brother-in-law shouted. "Open that fucking door if you got any balls!"

"Break it down if you can!"

Damien, furious, pounded on it even harder, and with Jerome's help, they both tried to shoulder their way in.

We finally heard a metallic noise when the lock

broke open. The door opened wide showing us something that petrified us with horror.

CHAPTER 62
Deep down inside

Summer 2008

WHEN HE REGAINED CONSCIOUSNESS, *a glint of light was coming through the shed's windows. A pallid light, the sun wasn't quite up yet. As it was the end of July, he thought it must be about five thirty in the morning.*

His cheek was lying on a wooden surface. Like an old hardwood floor. His eyelids were half-open, he didn't have enough strength to move, as if his body wasn't yet in gear, or out of gas. He didn't recognize the place, wondered where the heck he was, what he was doing on those unknown premises, in a type of renovated wooden garden shed.

He shivered, he was cold, his whole body was aching.

Then when he turned his head and saw his nude thighs, his pants and underwear pulled down to his ankles, he remembered. Traces of dried blood maculated his white skin.

He tried to get up while pulling his clothes back on, but teetered on his weak legs. Slowly but surely he got dressed but winced when the cloth of his jeans reached his buttocks.

Now he was invaded by shame.

He felt broken in his flesh, ripped apart deep down inside. Scarred, tarnished. A piece of shit. A total piece of shit.

Tears inundated his pale cheeks, he hiccupped with affliction and pain when he leaned against one of the legs of that oak table, rememorating the marbled veins of its planks.

Then he opened *the door of the shed, wrapping his arms around himself to warm up. Vapor was coming out of his mouth each time he took a breath. It was a misty morning. He recognized the yard where the party last night had taken place, remembered snippets of it. Alcohol, fiesta, pool, exhaustion, arms pulling him, masculine voices, raucous laughter, insults, blows and indelible bruises deep inside him.*

He didn't want to be seen that way, with filthy blood, tears and shame, so he snuck out the back of the yard, over a wooden fence, one that led to a cornfield.

When he got to his parents' house, they were still sleeping, so he unlocked the door, threw his clothing into the washing machine, added a few pieces of dark clothing to the load, pushed the button and rushed up to the bathroom next to his room. He wanted to erase the filth of the night under the scorching water, rinse his dishonor, try to delete the events of the past evening.

But he already knew that he'd never be able to forget his torturers. He understood that that summer night in 2008 would be a turning point in his life, one branded with the seal of infamy.

He finally got out, dried himself, put on some clean underwear and went to bed. All he wanted to do was to sleep and forget.

HE'D NEVER BE able to do that though. He'd never be the same again.

SINCE THAT NIGHT, he had been fomenting a fierce hatred towards all humanity and especially towards a small handful of people.

Firstly those four guys who'd walled him in alive, in dishonor. Last night, though he hadn't been totally lucid, he would be able to identify them, even though they were behind his back most of the time. He'd never forget them.

But he curiously targeted his seething hatred towards two other persons that in his mind were just as guilty as those four bastards who'd savagely fucked him, one after the other.

The sequence he'd drawn up in his wounded mind

was for him both logical and implacable. If this had happened to him, its cause was more profound in his mental schema.

A SYLLOGISM PUT itself in place in his scarred mind and body.

HE WAS MOLESTED because of his homosexual attractions. Attractions he'd unintentionally triggered himself as months and years went by.

HE'D CHOSEN that sexual penchant simply because it was easier for him, responding to the advances of an acquaintance he'd hung out with in the gym showers, instead of incessantly being systematically rejected by the opposite sex. First of all, that girl who haunted his daily erotic dreams ever since he was a teen, her inaccessible beauty, too perfect for a kid like him. A kid who was too ugly, too shy, too much of this and not enough of that.

IF THAT YOUNG girl never gave in to his advances, it was also because of that blond beefcake, that Patrick Swayze wannabe, the one the girl had finally said yes to.

. . .

He rested his case! What he wanted to prove, he'd already firmly established in his love-sick mind. He focused his pain and hatred on those two people: that idealized young girl and her beefcake. If he'd been raped that night, it was their fault!

As of that day, his sexual life — or absence of which — would only be experienced through that prism distorting reality.

During years, even decades to come, his thoughts and his acts would only be guided by that conviction, that belief he had deep down inside of him ever since that awful night back in the summer of 2008, in that wooden shed with its oak table.

He knew right then that he'd get revenge, one day or another.

He knew how to be patient.

Take time to plot that revenge.

So that it would blow up at the very moment he'd himself chosen.

CHAPTER 63

Unfortunate uncertainties

THE FIRST IMAGE my retina captured was the horrified face of my sister.

Sara horrified, Sara terrified, but Sara was alive!

Her disproportionately open eyes betrayed the horror she must have been feeling.

Our impetus pushed us inside that room with its wood paneled walls, but we ground to a halt when we discovered the interior.

The terrifying horror of it.

How can you bear the image of a wife, a sister, a sister-in-law being threatened with imminent and violent death?

THE MAN, camouflaged behind a mask, was holding her in front of him like a human shield. His right hand was covering her mouth and in his left hand he was holding a seven-inch-long sharp knife right against Sara's throat.

"No! Don't do it! Whoever you are, I'm begging you, let her go," I stammered, my voice broken by my sobs.

My big sister, who was being threatened to have her throat slit, was like that proverbial straw that broke the camel's back for me.

The man, hiding behind his leather mask, was sniggering like a madman. A cold, emotionless laugh, one that reminded me of Jack Nicholson in *Shining*, a movie that really impacted me when I'd seen it with my girlfriends when I was sixteen.

But *Shining* was fictitious...

That night, reality exceeded that horror film.

Damien began to approach his captive wife.

"One more step and ... *couic*! Like a stuck pig... Understand?" asked the masked man.

"Who are you?" Jerome asked. "Why don't you take that fucking mask off to talk to us? What are you hiding? You're ugly? Scar faced? Ashamed of what you're doing?"

"Zip it, newspaper guy! Shut up now! First of all you gotta know that you're just as responsible as all the others for what's happening here today."

His voice — just like his hand holding the knife — was trembling with excitement. Nonetheless, despite his tremolos, I was sure I'd already heard that voice someplace but couldn't manage to associate it with a name or a face. It rang some sort of bell, but which one?

Have you ever had that impression that you'd put your finger on some certainty, though you were unable to know if you had found that solution in your long-term memory or in some more recent event? That was what I was feeling.

"We know each other, don't we?"

More hyena-like laughter.

"Oh! Yes. We do know each other very well even..."

"So why are you hiding behind that mask?"

"Because I'm the one who decides. I'm the boss here, don't you agree?"

To prove those remarks, the man put his knife even closer to Sara's throat.

My poor sister tried to flee the scene she was an expiratory victim of by closing her eyes. She didn't want to see death approaching her. She was afraid to move, to try to get away, thinking he'd slit her throat before, and she'd die drowning in her own blood. The only possible escape for her was a mental one, and she closed her eyes.

"What I think is that you're afraid to kill her," I said, trying to provoke him. "You led us here, but after that you're hiding behind that ridiculous SM costume. Congratulations! You've got balls!"

What better way to get to a man's self-esteem than by attacking his virility? I was sure that would work.

"Don't worry Colombe, you'll see my face soon enough. Let me enjoy this moment. I've been waiting for it for such a long time. I'm surprised though that you haven't guessed who I am. I thought I was clear. Weren't my riddles precise enough? But you're here, you must have understood them."

"Let's stop playing now. Put that knife down and let Sara go. She's not a character in your story."

"That's what you say. Each piece of my puzzle has to perfectly fit with the others to make a perfect image. Your big sister is one of those pieces. Would you have come here to me Colombe, had I not had your sister as bait? I don't think so."

"Why her though?" I wanted to know.

It was time for that joker to show his cards so we could understand his motivation.

"And why not? Sometimes in life you have good luck and sometimes you have unfortunate uncertainties, as if some people were born under a lucky star and others weren't. You'll soon understand. Right now, I've got a question for you."

He was employing a saccharine tone, one that made me shiver, because I thought I'd already heard it. That underlying irony that I'd felt for the last few days.

Things were starting to gel in my little head, but I still couldn't believe the implications stemming from it. If what I was thinking was true, the duplicity of that man made me nauseous.

"And if I refuse to answer, I suppose you're still going to ask me it?"

"Spot on. I'm the *boss* now. I suffered from being *bossed* by others for too long. But all that's history. So my question: are you wondering why we're all together here exactly? Do you understand what that implies? Do you remember the summer of 2008?"

Of course I remembered now. As time went by, memories of it came back little by little, and I remembered events I'd occulted for nearly fifteen years. Because when I was sixteen, they really didn't concern me.

"I do. I remember a party at the end of summer. A whole bunch of us got together in a huge house that belonged to the parents of one of the girls from high school, in Aurillac. We had the house and the pool just for us, no parents there to supervise anything. There was music, people were dancing on the patio or messing around in the pool. They were laughing, drinking, swimming, smoking joints, it was the last big fiesta before it was time to go back to school again. A great evening…"

"Not great for everyone," the masked man cut me off. "See, according to the point of view you have, the same party could be a dream or a nightmare. For me it was the beginning of an endless nightmare. Even though you may say we're nearing the end."

"I don't understand how that concerns Sara and me. And even less Damien and Jerome who we didn't even know back then."

"I must admit that they're just collateral victims in this litigation between us."

"What litigation?" I shouted.

"I'm getting there. Hold your horses. You'll remember everything suddenly, Colombine…"

That nickname he suddenly used in circumstances like that destabilized me. Hardly anyone used that alias outside of my family.

"Don't call me that! I forbid you! Who the hell are you? Show us your face!" I screamed, out of control.

"You're right, Colombine. I'll take the mask off."

Turning talk into action, he took his hand off Sara's mouth and grabbed his leather mask at the bottom of his neck.

The mask began to unveil the bottom of his face, then inch by inch, his features.

Discovering the identity of that sick bully was a confirmation of my suspicions, mixed with both surprise and incomprehension.

It wasn't possible! Not him!

CHAPTER 64
Spitting it out

"BERTRAND?"

"Sure is!" my cousin replied laughing. "The one and only Bertrand Signol, as known as Bert, in flesh and blood! Bet you weren't expecting that one, huh?"

To tell you the truth, I had no idea what to expect anymore. My cousin, who had attended our wedding just a couple of days ago and who I trusted, even so much that I'd asked him to help us because of his skills in IT, had kidnapped my sister — his own cousin — and was threatening her with a sharp kitchen knife...

Next to me Jerome and Damien were also sick to their stomachs, their jaws clenched in wrath and hatred.

"Bertrand, what's wrong?" I tried to calm him. "We're all responsible adults here. You're going to put your knife down and let Sara go, and after that we'll talk, I promise. Okay? Don't do anything you'll regret for the rest of your life…"

"Can it! You wannabe psychologist! Who the hell are you preaching about regrets? Do you have any idea what happened to me right here fifteen years ago? And all of that was your fault, Colombe! Your fault! My life was destroyed forever in 2008, and it was because of you! So don't try to give me any lessons now, it's too late. You should have done something back then."

While speaking, he walked to the back of the room, dragging Sara who was sobbing openly.

"Bertrand, I don't understand. What should I have done? I have no idea what happened. Tell me…" I begged him. "Is there anything I can do now to repair it? Please, let your cousin go and we can talk this over. You know, the cops are coming and if you don't release her quickly, things could go downhill fast for you."

"I told you Colombine, it's too late now. The evil that was done can't be undone. I thought I'd get over it, but no, some things hurt your soul just as much as your heart and your body. Internal injuries that no one can see, though they're there, unforgettable."

While he was speaking, his grip on Sara seemed to loosen up a bit. The hand holding that knife dropped slowly as he went back in time, as he told them about his adolescence. Damien, Jerome and I all noticed this and were ready to pounce on him as soon as we had an opportunity to do so and preferred to allow him to spit it all out.

I let him continue.

"It was here, right in this very place, that I endured the worst humiliation and suffering in my entire life…"

During the following ten minutes, Bertrand told us the whole story, down to the smallest details of what happened to him that night in that wooden shed while others were having fun, a few hundred feet away from him, in the pool, in the house, and for some, in its bedrooms.

His terrible tale was finally over.

"Colombe, do you know what that incongruous object I left you in that plastic bag under the oak tree is?"

"It looks like a frying pan handle. But that blood on the end?"

"Don't panic, it's just some blood I got from a steak. A symbol so you'd understand what happened to me that night with that object that perforated… my soul… forever…"

When he had finished telling us that indelible episode of his past, out of breath, sweating, his voice broken and legs that could no longer support him, Bertrand let himself slide to the floor, dragging Sara in his wake. Now both of them were hugging each other in a corner of the shed, crying.

Jerome, Damien and I were petrified by the ignominy of his tale, one even worse as his rape had taken place right here, in front of us, right on that oak table he'd just described, on that floor where he spent the rest of that night, trembling with shame and pain, during that summer night back in 2008.

No one said a word.

Bertrand finally composed himself a bit and spoke, nearly in a whisper this time.

"And Colombe, all that was your fault."

"Seriously, my fault? I still don't understand you, Bert.

How can this be my fault? You have to explain yourself."

My cousin took a deep breath.

"You never wanted to go out with me because I was too ugly, isn't that true?"

I was unprepared for that question.

"What are you talking about, Bert?"

"The truth, Colombe. The fucking truth! I loved you. You couldn't ignore something like that. I was so in love with you. When I watched you in the gym with your leotards. When my eyes ate you alive on the banks of the river, when you wore your sexy swimsuit. When I admired your bewitching smile and beautiful eyes. Each time I saw you, all I could think of was approaching you, touching you, caressing you, kissing you. I dreamed of you each night. Of your body, your mouth, your breasts and everything else. I hurt myself by pleasuring myself each night, alone in my bed, alone with my frustrations as my bedmate. But of course, you never realized any of that, did you? You never even imagined an ounce of my despair. No, you never even saw fit to smile at me even once, to get close to me, just give me a simple kiss."

"Bertrand, I'm so sorry to hear all of that now. I don't know what to say."

"Why? Had I told you all of that earlier, things would have been different for us? Colombe, I didn't want your pity, I wanted your love."

"Bert, an impossible love. Don't forget, we're cousins."

"That never stopped people from loving each other. And incidentally, you seem to have forgotten a detail."

"What?"

"Pascal's your cousin too! Yet that didn't seem to bother you, did it?"

CHAPTER 65
The trigger

I SQUINTED, trying to conjure up memories.

"What's Pascal got to do with this?"

"Don't pretend to be astonished, Colombe. Ah! Unlike me, he was a good-looking guy. All the girls longed for him, with his cute angel face and blond hair, his muscles that he paraded around at the river in his trunks, or when he dove right into the pool from the high diving board! Yup, all those girls drooled over him, were ready to crawl at his feet to be chosen, to be the one whose cherry would be popped by that handsome blond male, that rooster in the barnyard chanting *cock-a-doodle-doo*, while walking in shit. And you, admit it, you drooled over him too. Even though you played hard-to-get for a while, you gave in to him, Colombe. Yet you two were also cousins! Don't deny it, I saw you!"

"Saw us do what?" I defended myself, even though the object of his offense dated back to a bygone era.

"I surprised you. I'm sure you don't remember, because that wasn't important for you. But me, I never forgot that day when I followed you on my old moped. You were on his scooter, hanging on to him, your arms wrapped around his waist, rubbing your nearly nude breasts against his back. You thought you were alone in the world when you went into the forest. But I was there, hiding behind the trees, and I saw you two. Kissing, making out. You didn't consider him a cousin when he was sucking on your nipples, bitch!"

"Shut the hell up now!" Jerome barked suddenly when he heard that insult.

He ran to Bertrand and Sara, his fists clenched. I tried to stop him, but he was too powerful. He ground to a halt though when my cousin suddenly got back up, lifting Sara up as if she were a feather, repositioning the blade of his knife against my sister's throat.

"One more step and I'll slit her throat!"

Jerome stopped, his fists and jaw clenched. Powerless against Bertrand's fury and insanity.

My cousin had plotted out his revenge for years. Our wedding must have been the trigger that sent him over the edge. That day, when he'd attended our wedding, Bertrand must have finally understood that I would now be permanently inaccessible. In that case though, why didn't he attack either Jerome or I directly? Why threaten Sara?

One more thing I didn't understand.

"But why didn't you direct your hatred towards

those guys who..." — I wanted to say raped you — "did that to you here in this shed?"

"Okay. You'll understand why we're here. It's a sequence of unfortunate events. For me. When you were sixteen, you had no qualms about rejecting me and throwing yourself into Pascal's arms. Back then I could have tried to beat him up. But I didn't have the balls to. But he was much stronger than me, plus I realized that your infatuation with him only lasted for a few scorching days. A relationship with a whiff of prohibition probably. Though you two split up, you didn't change your attitude towards me. You kept on pushing me away, humiliating me."

"But maybe another girl would have liked you," I pleaded. "You weren't that bad-looking you know. Plus there's always someone for everyone!"

"No! I wanted you. Only you. You were my goddess, my beauty, my living dream. And no, no other girls wanted me. So one day, in despair, maybe as a challenge too, I let myself give into a guy. I tried it... If that was all I could do... And people found out. They started calling me a faggot, a cocksucker, a homo. And it all went downhill from there. Exactly that summer and at that party right here. Those guys wanted to bust a gay person, and I was the only one there. What happened to me that night Colombe stemmed from your stubbornness of not accepting me as your boyfriend."

That accusation fell on me just like a black veil over a widow's face. I suddenly didn't have any energy left, I was assailed and overwhelmed by guilt I couldn't do anything about. I understood then that I had unwittingly been the person to trigger a terrible human tragedy, a secret and terrible wound that had never healed for my cousin.

"I'm so terribly sorry, Bertrand," was all that I could say before collapsing, pale, my eyes filled with tears.

It was once again silent, everyone was lost in their own thoughts, touched by their own pains. Everything was pending on what would necessarily happen sooner or later. The outcome to that tragedy.

That outcome was precipitated when the police suddenly entered the shed.

"Drop that knife, Signol!" yelled Captain Delahousse, pointing his service weapon towards Bertrand. He tightened his grip on Sara.

And strengthened his grip on the handle of his knife.

CHAPTER 66
A single second

THE FEW SECONDS following the arrival of the captain and his men went by as if they were in slow motion, though everyone moved in a minute amount of time.

Each of us in our own way.

There were shouts of surprise, fear, hatred and authority.

Chairs were knocked over, objects fell to the ground, dishes were broken.

Sara screamed, stuck in Bertrand's stranglehold, who, leaning against the wall at the back of the shed, was facing the cops.

The squad seemed to be composed of six men, including Delahousse, who, as the chief, stood in front of his colleagues.

The captain was still aiming his gun at the aggressor and his victim.

"I'm gonna slit her throat if you take one more

step," shouted Bertrand, his eyes bulging with the hatred and wrath he'd accumulated for years.

"Don't do anything stupid, Signol. You'll just make things worse for you."

"I could care less now! Do you understand that?" he shouted out.

Was he addressing everyone or just one of us in particular? Or himself? Or the ghost of his adolescence, the one that had suffered right here, fifteen years ago?

Delahousse advanced slowly, just like a feline who was prowling.

"It's too late," Bertrand continued. "I already died here in this room once, when I was sixteen. I'm not afraid of dying again. You can't kill a dead person! Shoot! Go ahead! Too afraid, huh?"

My cousin was sinking deeper into insanity right before our eyes. A soliloquy. His voice filled the room where each of us were watching that mind-boggling scene, stupefied, silent, and paralyzed with fear.

"I would have liked to finish my life with you in my arms, Colombe. Finish in beauty, a logical epilogue. Too bad, I'll have to do with your big sister, a bit too old for me back in the day, but today, she'll do the job."

What did he mean by those words? What was he planning on doing with Sara? That was when, with his free hand, he started to unbutton her jeans and slide them down, pushing her urine-covered panties down at the same time.

"Noooo!" Sara sobbed. "Not that."

She was struggling, but with his knife against her

throat, couldn't do much without risking being wounded, at the very least.

"You think I had the choice back in 2008 when those guys ripped my jeans off? Now it's your turn."

"Stop that right now, Signol!" the captain bellowed. "Or I will shoot!"

"You wouldn't do that sweetie," replied Bertrand ironically.

Delahousse caught my eye and made a miniscule movement I immediately understood.

THE NEXT SECOND would be crucial.

Sometimes a mere second can transform lives...

In that same second:

I shouted out: "Get down, Sara!"

Delahousse pulled the trigger. One bullet.

Hitting Bertrand, with his bloodshot eyes and mouth hanging open with surprise.

Sara was splashed with blood and fainted.

Right before Bertrand collapsed on her.

And the knife fell to the floor with a spooky metallic clang.

OUR NIGHTMARE WAS OVER.

CHAPTER 67

The facts

AFTER A FEW DAYS in the hospital, Bertrand went to the police station to be interviewed by Captain Delahousse.

His wound in his shoulder had neutralized him without endangering his life, nor the life of his prisoner.

Whenever possible, the policeman preferred to save lives, even those of the worst criminals.

It's always better to try to understand the explanations perps give to try to comprehend their motivations and how they went about committing their crimes. Not leaving any questions up in the air.

Bertrand Signol and Captain Delahousse were in his office, and the policeman had to admit he nearly admired his prowess.

"Signol, you're pretty good! Taking part in the cyber-investigators' team and fooling your cousin by making her suspect her other cousin… That was perfectly Machiavellian, congrats! You understood that the best way to draw attention away from you was to immerse yourself in the loop of victims of your own crime."

"When you've got talent," Bertrand replied ironically.

"Don't be a smartass! Tell me how you were always one step ahead of everyone, of us and of your cousin."

Bertrand Signol made a comical face before answering.

"Well, might as well admit everything. It can't get any worse. Everything started the day Colombe and Jerome got married. A perfect evening for them, and for me. I'm sure you can conceive that the newlyweds were talking to everyone, paying attention to every little detail, obsessed with making that truly 'the best day of their lives.' A perfect wedding reception and party. While they were busy, it was easy for me to pilfer their cell phones and install an undetectable spyware app in them that I'd need in the next few days. Just a few minutes in the cloak room while they were having their first dance as newlyweds under the admirative eyes of all their guests. No one paid any attention to me. You actually could say that that sums up my whole life: I've always been transparent, insignificant in the eyes of others, a nothing, a no one."

"Skip your victimization. Let's stick to the facts. What did you do with that spyware?"

"Yes, sir! Very simple. With that software I was able to follow them using a GPS geolocalization function. I always knew where they were, and that made it easy for me to remain a step ahead of everyone. I had time to prepare. And I didn't just know their positions. That little virtual spy also gave me access to all their conversations, text messages, WhatsApp, Messenger, and all that. Also recordings of their audio phone conversations. A gem, I highly recommend it for you."

"You are aware that this is totally illegal."

"Not that illegal. It's authorized for parents who want to keep track of their kids or know if they're chatting with sexual predators or other scumbags. Also practical for husbands whose wives are cheating on them. If you want, I can recommend it to Damien… In my opinion, this is in the public interest and should be mandatory!"

"Calm down. Keep on explaining. What did you get from spying on your cousin and her husband?"

"That was the best part. From my point of view obviously. I had so much fun! Following their conversations when they were racking their brains to find an answer to one of my enigmas. I gotta even admit that I listened in on their intimate little phone conversations. So delightful to be omnipresent and omniscient! Just like the author of a novel, the person who knows everything, sees everything. Ah! I would have loved to be an author! But not everyone has that gift. Anyway, the phone calls and text messages — both the ones they sent and received — from Colombe and Jerome, came directly to me, including yours, Captain... So I knew exactly what progress you were making. I knew if you were getting close to me or if I still had a lot of wiggle room. Pure pleasure!"

"Enough of that. You did the same thing then to follow Sara and her lover?"

"Oh! That was a particularly exquisite episode," sneered Bertrand, thrilled to elaborate. "Let me just get off the track here a bit, Captain. You have to understand that to begin with, I wasn't targeting Sara. It just happened, and it was thanks to Colombe and Jerome. They were the ones who tipped me off when they mistakenly interpreted the poem I'd written for them. Those two, they really were studious with their Bible verses! And it happened at just the right time. So I began there, I allowed them to do their thing, then I followed them remotely when they flew to Marseille and then drove to Rousset. At the same time, still thanks to my spyware — it can be installed remotely — I was able to access Sara's phone and discover what she'd said to her lover, that Erich Elstrom who was so nostalgic of the Nazi regime. And from there I accessed that wannabe Nazi's phone, and I was able to track that illegitimate couple to Verdon Park, to his little hideaway, and then all I had to do was surprise them there."

"And then take Sara to the village where you lived when you were kids. Was that improvisation too?"

"No, that part was planned. That way I'd be able to

force Colombe to come to that shed in the backyard of that villa where all that atrocious stuff happened to me. A way of staging my revenge and tying up loose ends. Otherwise Colombe would have been much more careful and wouldn't have run off like that. But with her big sister as a prisoner whose life was being threatened, I knew she wouldn't hesitate for even a second. And I even had fun improvising a bit before leaving Verdon Park."

"I'm listening."

"The paper you found in the jacket Sara forgot, what she wrote," Bertrand sneered. "Under duress, of course. A last-minute idea to cover up my tracks. So that the investigators would be doubtful. I imagine my ruse didn't last very long, but it was so much fun. Like I was starring in some crime fiction, scattering false clues to hold up the investigation!"

"And you never thought we'd catch you?"

"Never! Remember, I was the one leading the waltz and pulling the strings. Plus with all the layers of protection I'd accumulated from the dark web, I was protected. And was I ever surprised when Colombe suggested that I work with the police, Captain. The ultimate paradox, don't you agree? The criminal was a member of the investigators' team. Like a fox in the henhouse. I was working at my pace remotely, directing suspicions towards Pascal, that guy Colombe had preferred back in 2008, — a little supplementary revenge that helped me confuse your investigation even more — while holding Sara right here. Killing three birds with one stone, if I can put it like that. Ingenious, don't you agree?"

"Signol, that's a joke I really don't appreciate. Nutjobs like you shouldn't be running free in society."

"I did understand that you didn't like my sense of humor, Captain."

"One more thing, Signol. Did you have anything to do with Suzanne's death?"

"Excuse me? Captain, I don't even know how you can imagine a thing like that concerning me! I'm outraged. A man like me attacking an old defenseless lady, really! But I'd like to reassure you on one point. Using my spyware, I can guarantee something that will save you time. The suspicions you had about that taxi driver, the one who drove her back to her room, the one who went to her funeral and who drove Colombe and Jerome to the airport in Merignac, are unfounded. His GPS tracker proves that he didn't go to the old person's home that night when Suzanne died. I guess it was just her time, for that old grandma... Unless I missed something. See Captain, right up to the end I'm of invaluable assistance, admit it."

"I'm not admitting a thing."

"Will that be all then?" Bertrand Signol asked provocatively.

"Till your trial, yes. And in the meanwhile, we'll try to shed some light on what happened to Suzanne and you... you'll have time to think things over behind bars. Anything else you'd like to add?"

Bertrand got up, smiling. He paced around in the

room, and when he arrived at the door, he turned around.

"A few useful tips for you: always watch out for taxi drivers and mailmen. Check the content of your cell phones every once in a while. You never know who could be listening in to what you're saying..."

Epilogue

IN THE DAYS following that dramatic episode after our wedding, little by little we were able to overcome our trauma, thanks to psychological assistance. My sister and brother-in-law also needed it. Slowly but surely the couple reconsolidated after they'd both lost their way during the months preceding Sara's fugue with her lover and her kidnapping.

Those painful events in the garden shed in Thiezac would undoubtedly haunt us for a long time.

Pascal, that poor innocent taxi driver, went back to his humdrum life and finally allowed his rescue dog to live with him comfortably upstairs. Her life in captivity thus ended for her when her master became aware of how much she must have suffered alone downstairs.

As for our cousin Bertrand, he had been incarcerated until his trial would take place. He'd be tried for various charges such as intimidation, harassment, kidnapping, sequestration, attempted homicide and false accusations. He was looking at a very long prison sentence. I felt more pity for him than hatred. His youth and adult life had been an unhappy and tragic one, he had been morally destroyed. Retrospectively I felt sorry for him more than accusing him.

∽

A FEW WEEKS later Jerome and I finally granted ourselves a pleasure most newlyweds enjoy: having a real honeymoon.

We'd decided to treat ourselves to a three-week trip in the United States, going from the east to the west coast. For the moment we were staying in the Acadia National Park, which was a small peninsula in Maine, a place that one of my favorite authors, the immense Stephen King, loves and lives not far from there.

Sitting on the rocks at the foot of Bass Harbor Lighthouse, serene, soothed by the naturally peaceful lapping of the waves, Jerome and I were contemplating the Atlantic Ocean.

Over the horizon, straight east, we were not missing Europe a bit. On the other side of that vast ocean, Biscarrosse, Rousset, Thiezac and their torments were finally *out of sight, out of mind*.

We tried to cure our psychological wounds by distancing ourselves from them.

Just enjoying the scenery was presently enough to make us happy. We didn't even find it necessary to disturb this peaceful moment by speaking.

"*Love isn't looking in each other's eyes, it's looking together in the same direction,*" as Antoine Saint-Exupéry wrote in *The Little Prince*.

That quote fit us to a T.

WE LOVED MAINE. It was the beginning of a trip we'd never forget. A peaceful one.

But it was also one where we made unsettling discoveries that sparked our natural journalistic curiosity.

But that's another story, one that maybe one day, Jerome or I could write a book about…

THE END

A few words from the author

This is usually a useful and pleasant part of the book for me.

One where I thank all the people who contributed, in one way or another, from near or far, to the birth of the novel you've just read.
    Today though, just after having written THE END, I'm going to depart from this rule and I hope you'll forgive me for it, because my heart will be expressing itself here.

As I write these few lines, Helene, my Granny, my Grandma, the person I dedicated this novel to, is hovering between life and death at the hospital. Just a few weeks ago, she was still flooding our hearts with her bright laughter, as usual showing her generosity, her kindness, her love.

Her body only took a few days to say STOP, to fog her brain, to become unrecognizable, for her to be unable to recognize us. As if she now has become merely an empty shell.

All of us, her loved ones, feel that she is losing her race against death.

And I suddenly have a very bad feeling stemming from coincidences that are too huge to be true, something readers sometimes say about the twists in our novels.

Yet, the facts are there, unsettling ones.

When I wrote my first novel, *True Blood Never Lies*, between 2008 and 2010, I described the death of Leo's father, then the birth of his son. And strangely, in 2009 my father died prematurely, and my son was born.

In this novel, I wrote about the death of Colombe's grandmother in her bed in her senior residence... And now my Granny is about to move into a senior residence... or not... depending on whether she wins her race against death.

You see, I'm afraid of becoming a prophet of gloom and doom. I'm afraid, just like Demiurge, the name Platon gave to the creator of the universe, that my words could become reality.

When you read these words — as books have the advantage of being eternal — perhaps my Granny Helene will have already left to join her dear Mickey and her dear Veve...

I'd like all three of them to know, if they hear me, if they see me, that I'll always miss them.

Sébastien, alias Nino...
    January 28, 2022

By the same author

THE KAREN BLACKSTONE SERIES
Into Thin Air (2022) (*Winner of the Cuxac d'Aude Favorite Novel, 2023 / Finalist in the Loiret Crime Award, 2023*)
I Want Mommy (2023) (*N°1 in Amazon Storyteller sales 2023*)
The Lost Son (2023)
Alone (2024)
Volume 5 to be published in 2025

THE BASTERO SERIES
French Riviera – *One Too Many Brothers* (2017) (*Winner of the Indie award Ilestbiencelivre 2017*)
Perfect crime? (2020)
Bloody Bonds (2022)

BY THE SAME AUTHOR

OTHER NOVELS
True Blood Never Lies (2022)
Thirty Seconds Before Dying (2021)

French Riviera – One Too Many Brothers

The first two volumes in the Colombe Deschamps and Jerome Bastaro series..

In the Lacassagne family, everyone's got their own little secret.

Summer of 1986

In the Baie des Anges, Pierre-Hugues, the oldest son in the Lacassagne family, drowns while sailing with his brother and sister.

Summer of 2016

At nearly eighty years old, Charles Lacassagne, a rich property developer in Nice, is thinking of handing over the reins of his empire to his children. At the same time, he contacts a Parisian journalist, Jerome Bastaro, to write his biography.

But Jerome will quickly find out that the foundations of this highly successful family are fragile: drama, secrets and lies play an important part in the Lacassagne family's past and present.

He soon is faced with a dilemma : stick to his contract and like a good little boy tell the story that Charles is expecting or follow his instincts and investigate to write "the truth about the Lacassagne case".

Perfect Crime?

They were expecting a dream vacation on a tropical island... But...

Colombe Deschamps and Jerome Bastaro, our two journalists, fly to Guadeloupe to spend a dream vacation of a lifetime in a bungalow in an upscale resort, with a small group of fellow vacationers.

But Death knocks on the resort's doors. Undetectable and relentless...

They don't notice a thing though the solution is right there, below their eyes.

... will they witness a perfect crime?

After the immense success of French Riviera, Nino S. Theveny, Sebastien Theveny's American pen name, writes another novel starring the journalists-investigators his readers love and appreciate. After French Riviera, this time the author sends them to the Caribbean. At the same time, he sends his readers off in a narrative bet where he insidiously gives them all the keys to solve this diabolical mystery.

Who am I?

Nino S. Theveny is one of France's leading indie authors. He's married and has two children. In 2019 he was laid off from a multinational company and decided to make the most of his newly found liberty, turning to writing, his passion, which is now his day job.
With 15 books published to date, Nino S. Theveny has over 220,000 readers. Translated into English, Spanish, Italian, and German, his thrillers are appreciated throughout the entire world.
With his fourteen-year-old son, he has also co-authored a thriller for young adults which was published in March, 2024.

Printed in Dunstable, United Kingdom